The Privet Hedge

J. E. Buckrose

Alpha Editions

This edition published in 2024

ISBN 9789362513656

Design and Setting By
Alpha Editions
www.alphaedis.com
Email - info@alphaedis.com

Contents

Chapter I
The Cottage

At the far end of Thorhaven towards the north was a little square house surrounded by a privet hedge. It had a green door under a sort of wooden canopy with two flat windows on either side, and seemed to stand there defying the rows and rows of terraces, avenues and meanish semi-detached villas which were creeping up to it. Behind lay the flat fields under a wide sky just as they had lain for centuries, with the gulls screaming across them inland from the mud cliffs, and so the cottage formed a sort of outpost, facing alone the hordes of jerry-built houses which threatened to sweep on and surround it.

The ladies who lived at the Cottage had once been nicknamed the Misses Canute—which showed how plainly all this could be seen, as a sort of symbol, by anyone in the least imaginative; though it was a rather unsatisfactory curate from Manchester who actually gave them the name. No one felt surprised when he afterwards offended his bishop and went into the motor business, for he suffered from that constitutional ability to take people as seriously as they wished to be taken, which is so bad for any career.

Thus the curate departed, but his irreverence lived on after him for quite a long time, because many people like a mild joke which every one must see at once—which is ready-made—and for which they cannot be held responsible. So this became for a little while the family jest of Thorhaven, in no way spoiled by the fact that one sister had married a man called Bradford and was now a widow, while the other retained the paternal Wilson.

The two ladies were walking together on this twenty-sixth of March, by the side of the privet hedge which divided their garden from the large field beyond and hid from them everything which they did not care to see.

Miss Ethel's name was entirely unsuited to her, but she had received it at a period when Ethels were as thick as blackberries in every girls' school of any pretensions; and she was not in the very least like any Miss Amelia out of a book, though she possessed an elder sister and had reached fifty-five without getting married. On the contrary, she carried her head with great assurance on her spare shoulders, put her hair in curling pins each night as punctually as she said her prayers, and wore a well-cut, shortish tweed skirt with sensible shoes. Her face was thin and she had a delicately-shaped, rather long nose, together with a charmingly-shaped mouth that had grown compressed and lost its sweetness. A mole over her right eyebrow accentuated her habit of twitching that side of her face a little when she was nervous or excited.

But she was calm now, walking there with her sister, enjoying the keen air warmed with sunshine which makes life on such a day in Thorhaven sparkle with possibilities.

"I'm glad," she said, "that we decided not to clip the hedge. It has grown up until it hides that odious Emerald Avenue entirely from the garden."

"I can still see it from my bedroom window all the same," said Mrs. Bradford.

"Don't look out of your window, then!" retorted Miss Ethel sharply.

"You take care of that," said Mrs. Bradford. "You have made the short blinds so high that I can scarcely see over them."

"Do you want the people in those awful little houses to see you undressing?" demanded Miss Ethel.

"They couldn't—not unless they used a telescope or opera glasses," said Mrs. Bradford. And she managed to convey, by some subtle inflexion of voice and expression—though she was a dull woman—that if you had been married, you were not so pernickitty about such things; and, finally, that if Emerald Avenue cared to go to that trouble it was welcome, because she remained always invested with the mantle of Hymen.

As a matter of fact, she had—in a way—spent her life for some years in echoing that romantic declaration of the lady in the play: "I have lived and loved." Only she had never said anything so vivid as that—she simply sat down on the fact for the rest of her life in a sort of comatose triumph.

Her husband had been a short, weasely man of bilious temperament; still, he sufficed; and his death at the end of two years from whooping-cough only added to Mrs. Bradford's complacency. She came back home again to the Cottage, feeling as immeasurably superior to her unmarried sister as only a woman of that generation could feel, who had found a husband while most of her female relatives remained spinsters. She at once caused the late Mr. Bradford's photograph to be enlarged—the one in profile where the eyebrows had been strengthened, and the slight squint was of course invisible—and she referred to him in conversation as "such a fine intellectual-looking man." After a while, she began to believe her own words more and more thoroughly, so that at the end of ten years she would not have recognized him at all had he appeared in the flesh.

"At any rate," she remarked, "our field won't be built over."

"No, thank goodness!" assented Miss Ethel emphatically, her left eyebrow twitching a little. "The Warringborns will never sell their land, whatever other people do. I remember grandfather telling us how he was ordered out of the room by old Squire Warringborn when he once went to suggest buying this field. Oh, no; the Warringborns won't sell. Not the least fear of that."

But she only talked in this way because she was afraid—trying to keep her heart up, as she saw in her mind's eye that oncoming horde of yellowish-red houses.

Before Mrs. Bradford could reply about the Warringborns, there came a sound of voices in the great field which stretched park-like beyond the privet hedge. "Butcher Walker putting some sheep in, I expect," said Mrs. Bradford. "He has the lease of it now."

But even as she spoke, her heavy jaw dropped and she stood staring. Miss Ethel swerved quickly round in the same direction, and her pale eyes focused. Neither of them uttered a sound as they looked at the square board which rose slowly above the privet hedge. They could not see the pole on which it was supported from that position in the garden, and so it appeared to them like a banner upheld by unseen hands.

"Well," said Mrs. Bradford at last, "we mustn't clip the hedge this year, that's all. Then——"

"Hedge!" cried Miss Ethel. "What's the use of talking about the hedge when our home is spoilt? Look! Read!" She pointed to that square object which flaunted now in all its glaring black and white newness—a blot against the grey sky.

FOR SALE
FOR THE ERECTION OF VILLAS AND
BUNGALOWS
APPLY MESSRS. GLATT & WILSON

Miss Ethel could not have felt deeper dismay if the square notice board on the pole had been indeed held aloft by the very Spirit of Change itself, with streaming hair still all aflame from rushing too closely past a bursting sun. Only those who hate change as she did could ever understand her dismay.

"We shall be driven out of our house. We shall have to leave," she said, very pale. "After all these years, we shall have to go. We *can't* stand all their nasty little back ways!"

"Where are we to go to?" said Mrs. Bradford. She paused a moment. "It's the same everywhere. Besides, the houses are not built yet."

There was nothing for them to do but to turn their backs on the board and walk quietly away, filled with that aching home-sickness for the quiet past which thousands of middle-aged people were feeling at that moment all over Europe. Everything was so different, and the knowledge of it gave to Miss Ethel a constant sense of exasperated discomfort, like the ache of an internal disease which she could not forget for a moment.

"I expect," she said after a while, "that Mrs. Graham will once more tell us to let ourselves go with the tide and not worry. Thank God, I never was a supine jelly-fish, and I can't start being one now."

"She was talking about servants," said Mrs. Bradford, who was troubled, but not so troubled, because she took things differently. "I expect she only meant we should never get another like Ellen; but we can't expect to do so after having her for eleven years."

"No. We are lucky to have Ellen's niece coming. But I wish she were a little older," said Miss Ethel. "Nineteen is very young."

"Yes," replied Mrs. Bradford, letting the conversation drop, for she was not very fond of talking. And in the silence they looked back; and to both of them nineteen seemed a rather ridiculous and foolish age—even for a servant, who is supposed to be rather young.

Then Miss Ethel began again—talking on to try and banish the insistent vision in her mind's eye of that square board over the privet hedge, which she knew herself foolish to dwell upon. "I wish Caroline had not lived with Ellen's sister and gone out as a day-girl to that little grocer's shop in the Avenue. I'm afraid that may have spoilt her. But it is Caroline or nobody. We may want a sensible middle-aged maid, but in these days it isn't what you want—it's what you can get."

Mrs. Bradford nodded; and again they felt all over them that resentful home-sickness for the past.

"One thing—we must begin as we mean to go on," said Miss Ethel. "If mistresses were only firmer there would never be such ridiculous proceedings as one hears about; but they are so afraid of losing maids that they put up with anything. No wonder the girls find this out and cease to have any respect for them. Look at Mrs. Graham! A latch-key allowed, and no caps or aprons. That's swimming with the tide, with a vengeance."

"There's no fear of Caroline wanting anything of that sort," said Mrs. Bradford. "Ellen's sister, Mrs. Creddle, is as steady as Ellen."

"She'd need to be, with four children on her hands, and a husband like one of those coco-nuts at Hull fair that have the husk partly left on," said Miss Ethel. "I never could understand how a nice-looking girl, such as Mrs. Creddle was then, came to marry such a man."

Mrs. Bradford looked down at her fat hands and smiled a little, seeming to see things in the matrimonial philosophy that no spinster was likely to understand. Then after opening the door they both turned again, from force of long habit, to look across the garden, and saw the square board more plainly now than they had done when close under the hedge. It stood there in the midst of the grass field—as if it were leading on—while in the distance the wind from the east was blowing the smoke like flags from the long row of chimney-tops in Emerald Avenue.

At last Miss Ethel said with a sort of doubtful hopefulness, as if keeping her courage up before those advancing hordes: "Perhaps nobody will want to buy the land there. Always heard it was boggy."

Mrs. Bradford shook her head silently and went in, followed by her sister: in a world where all things were now odiously possible, one had to take what came and make the best of it.

But Miss Ethel already experienced the faint beginning of a state of suspense which was never to cease, day or night, though at times she was not conscious of it. She fancied that every person who crossed the field was an intending buyer, and woke with a start when the old wardrobe gave the sudden "pop!" in the night to which she had been long accustomed, thinking for the moment that she heard the first stroke of a workman's hammer. In truth she was run down with doing most of the work of the house since Ellen's departure to look after an invalid mother, besides suffering from several severe colds during the winter, so that the possibility of new houses being built close at hand had got on her nerves, and gained an almost ridiculous importance.

She and her sister had thought, like so many others, that they could escape change by living in one place, but it had followed them, as it always inexorably does. Shut their eyes as they might, they had to see neighbours leaving, neighbours dying. And even those who remained did not continue the same. One day Miss Ethel was obliged to notice how grey little Mrs. Baker at the newspaper shop was going—and that brought to mind that she had been married thirty years come Christmas. Thirty years! It seemed incredible that so much of life had slipped almost imperceptibly away.

All the same, she *ached* to stand still. She simply could not realize that perhaps some other generation would look back on hers as she did on the past. One Saturday the following lines in the local corner of the *Thorhaven and County Weekly Budget*—between an advertisement of a new poultry food and a notice of a fine goat for sale—did express a little of her state of mind, though they were written by a retired schoolmistress in the detested Emerald Avenue—

The world is full of hurry and change,
And everything seems so new and strange;
But it's stranger still that one of these days
They'll call what *we're* doing, "the dear old ways."

It remained incredible, whatever reason might tell her, that anything more iconoclastic could be hidden in the womb of time than the Warringborns selling their land and Mrs. Graham letting her maid go to dances on the promenade, with a powdered face and a latch-key.

Chapter II
Caroline

The promenade at Thorhaven was reached by a short, wide street where a wind blew always, even on the stillest days, and the hall in which the young people of the little town danced weekly stood straight in front of the approaching visitor, entirely blocking out the view and the sea. Some people thought this must have happened by accident, but others felt sure that some subtle brain on the Urban District Council had correctly gauged what the cherished Visitor—the Council naturally thought of him or her with a capital letter—really considered a most important feature of an up-to-date seaside resort.

The hall itself was a glass erection, and it was in design so like those miniature forcing-houses placed over cherished plants in a garden border that no one with any imagination could avoid feeling momentarily that it must have been placed there by some good-natured giant—well disposed towards Thorhaven—for the express purpose of making the Visitor "come on" during the seaside holiday.

At the entrance gate stood a sort of sentry-box where two girls sat in turn from ten to ten. These girls were chosen by an optimistic Committee who hoped they would possess amiability, endurance, and particularly a gift for remembering faces: because the inhabitants of Thorhaven felt that their promenade was first of all *theirs*—and that no assistant employed at the gate had a right *not* to know them by sight when they entered the precincts for which their own rates and taxes had paid. Therefore—though this led to occasional abuse—it was found necessary to municipal harmony to let inhabitants in "on the nod."

Two young ladies of blameless reputation who were supposed to possess the required gifts had already been engaged for the season. One had filled the post before, and another was new to the job but promising. But time and love wait on the convenience of none—not even so important a body as the Thorhaven Amusements Committee—and girl number one unexpectedly ran away with a ship's engineer, while girl number two developed bronchial tendencies which made the pay-box unsuitable. So there were none.

On this bleak, bright day at the end of March, the pay-box with the wind howling round it did indeed look a bracing place to spend the day in, nor was it by any means an object which any would be likely to watch for five minutes at a stretch in a strong north-easter. But that was exactly what a palish girl with freckles on her nose had been doing for that length of time, and so intent was she on her own thoughts that she held a loose strand of hair in her hand instead of tucking it under her cap while she stood there with eyes fixed intently on the little ticket-window.

Her eyes were light—a greenish-grey flecked with gold—but they were very bright with dark lashes and themselves appeared quite dark when she was moved or excited. Nobody ever seemed to know what colour they were, not even the young fellow with whom she had been "going" ever since she left school, and she was generally considered in Thorhaven to have brown eyes.

After some time she withdrew that eager gaze, swerved round as if on a pivot, and started at a tremendous pace up the short, windy street that led to the main road. "I'll do it!" she said to herself—young lips tightly pressed, and nails biting into her palms even through her gloves. "I don't care what aunt says. It's my life, not hers. It's nobody's business but my own."

At the corner she stood a moment, searching the long grey road that led to the church. After a while she saw a cart in the distance laden with parcels and boxes, and she began to run after it, calling as she went: "Hi! Mr. Willis! Mr. Willis! Please stop! I want my box back. I don't want it taken to Miss Wilson's."

Mr. Willis pulled up and looked back over his shoulder. He had a weather-beaten, humorous face and was very slow in his habit of speech. "Quarrelled with Miss Ethel before you get there?" he said. "That's a bit quicker work than usual. Servant lasses generally let me get their boxes over the doorstep before they want to come away, even nowadays."

"Well, I don't mean to live servant with anybody," said Caroline, frowning. "I've changed my mind all of a sudden because I only heard of another opening this morning. I never wanted to go to the Cottage; it was all Aunt Creddle. She always promised I should, when I got to be nineteen, and I didn't seem as if I could get out of it."

"Well!" He jerked the reins. "Appears to me you might have spread some of your thinking over the last four years instead of doing it all since breakfast this morning." And he added over his shoulder: "I'm to leave your box at Mrs. Creddle's, as I come back, then?"

"Yes, please," said Caroline, fumbling with her purse.

Mr. Willis's face wrinkled up into many little lines and bosses as he looked down at her running beside the cart, with her coppers held out. "No, no. Put it in your pocket. You told me to take your box to Miss

Wilson's. I don't want money for work I haven't done." Then he whipped up the horse so that she could not keep pace with it.

She paused to take breath and stood looking after him, thinking it was no wonder Dan Willis had never got on in the world; but she did not know how many things in the world he enjoyed which people who must hunt the last farthing all the time are obliged to miss. He was indeed a happy bachelor, lodging over a little bread shop in the old part of the village, and his sixty years sat lightly on him because he had always found so much to see and to admire in the streets of Thorhaven.

But as Caroline turned to hurry down Emerald Avenue she immediately forgot all about him, for in nearly every house some acquaintance was making ready for the advent of the Visitor—either hanging curtains or washing covers or standing furniture outside to beat—and she could have written a most valuable book entitled "Hint to Lodging Seekers." She possessed recondite, first-hand information, such as no outsider can know; as, for instance, the more white mats, spotless covers and antimacassars in April, the more stains and flies towards the end of August. But fortunately for the few slatterns in Thorhaven, she did not use her power.

Now she was racing in a whirl of emotion down Emerald Avenue and round the next turn into Pearl Terrace, where her aunt Mrs. Creddle lived. Strangers wondered to see the newer streets in Thorhaven all named after precious stones, but the reason was simple enough. A member of the Council had been inspired one warm June evening after three bottles of ginger-beer to name the first of these red rows of houses Cornelian Crescent. But that bold flight of fancy exhausted the afflatus, and it seemed easier to go on to Sapphire Road than to think of anything fresh. Now— after a lapse of years—Thorhaven's city fathers had begun to be proud of this street nomenclature, and to believe they had meant it from the very first.

Number 10 Pearl Terrace was a house on the north side of the road, and Caroline had been "day-girl" with the wife of a small grocer just round the corner from the age of fifteen and a half to the present time. Before she went there at eight and after her return at six, she had helped Mrs. Creddle during the crises constantly recurring in a family of four little girls under twelve years old. Indeed, as her aunt said, she formed another example of good coming out of evil—for evil it seemed, when the Creddles had been obliged to take in Caroline among their increasing brood after the death of her father and mother.

Not that there had ever been any question about it. "You couldn't let the poor little lass go to the workhouse," said Mrs. Creddle when anyone spoke to her on the subject. "Bless you, we've never missed the bit she used to eat before she began to make aught, and she's earned her keep with us over and over again since then."

Mr. Creddle also expressed the same meaning, though in different terms, when pals ventured with a smile to hint that he had lasses enough under his roof without getting in any from outside. "That's my business," he would say. "I don't see as anybody has a right to pass a remark. I'd rather have four lasses than a red nose, anyway."

If the person addressed happened to possess the outward and visible signs of alcoholic excess, so much the worse for him—Mr. Creddle was touchy on the subject of his family and did not wish to please. His own nose was slightly rubicund, but it was solely owing to the east winds which constantly blew across it as he worked for the Council on the long roads near the sea; for he was a sober man, and when he did have a glass of beer on a Saturday night, he brought it home in a jug to share with his wife.

For years, indeed, when the babies were arriving, that was their only little festival from week's end to week's end. They would stand the jug on the table, and Mrs. Creddle would bring out some freshly baked "pie"; with thick crust above and below, and apples or currants and sugar, or gooseberries inside; and with the house all clean for Sunday, they would take their hour of ease late on Saturday night.

So Caroline had been brought up in an atmosphere of kindness, though Mr. Creddle had once threatened to strap her if she ran about with the lads again after dark. He had caught her racing with streaming hair round some half-built houses in Emerald Avenue, among a party of boys who ought to have been in bed, and his brief comments as he escorted her home were Elizabethan and to the point. Oddly enough, they burnt deeper into her mind than the whole of Mrs. Creddle's cautious advice.

All that, however, was long ago. Now—demure and slim—Caroline would no more have thought of racing round half-built houses at night than Mrs. Creddle herself. But she flung open the front door of Number 10 with the same certainty of warm interest she had always felt on entering that house, for Mrs. Creddle might be "put out," unhappy, anxious—but never coldly indifferent.

"Aunt!" called Caroline from the foot of the stairs in the excited voice which she strove to keep calm.

Mrs. Creddle emerged from a bedroom, with her usual air of being a little too warm, whatever the weather, and her clear-skinned, jolly face a little perturbed. "What's the matter, Carrie? You know Miss Ethel's expecting you. You ought to be there by now."

Caroline drew back a pace, then let her missile fly. "I aren't——" But even in this stress of emotion she paused from force of habit to correct her speech—"I'm not going to Miss Wilson's."

"What!" Mrs. Creddle came down the stairs with the peculiar buoyancy of active stout people. "I've just sent your box. Whatever are you talking about, Carrie?"

"I met Mr. Brook—he's the one that has to do with the Amusements Committee: and he said if I applied for Maggie Wake's job, I should get it. They want somebody steady and respectable that knows how to behave."

"But you can't apply for it!" said Mrs. Creddle, breathing sharply as if from the impact of an actual blow. "You've promised for years to go to Miss Wilson's when Ellen left, and they've waited for you ever since November. You *can't* behave like this to them now, Carrie. I can understand your being tempted, but you can't do it. You promised faithful."

"No, I didn't," said Caroline. "I never promised anything. It was you that promised for me. And I always hated the thought of living in, and being tied up at nights in their old kitchen; only you and Aunt Ellen fixed it all up when I was a kid, and I somehow never thought of going against you. It seemed one of the things that had to be—like putting your hair up and such like—but I never wanted to do it my own self."

"Well, you can't run back now," said Mrs. Creddle. "After all that Miss Ethel and Mrs. Bradford have done for us in the past, I should be ashamed to think of such a thing. Why, this very dress I have on came from Mrs. Bradford, and your blouse was made from a print skirt of Miss Ethel's. And when you had whooping cough, they sent jelly and oranges and I don't know what. I don't understand how you can want to behave so badly to them, Carrie."

"Oh, I've not forgotten all that!" said Carrie, working herself up into a defiant rage because she wanted to feel a counter-irritant to a secret uneasiness which lurked at the bottom of her mind. "But spare food and old clothes ought not to buy a girl, body and soul. Anyway, I price myself higher than that. I'm not going to sacrifice a job I fancy, and thirty shillings a week, to be general servant to those two old women, and that's flat."

"But the ticket-collecting only lasts until the end of September," urged Mrs. Creddle, flushed and perturbed. "What shall you do then?"

"I don't know," said Caroline. "I mean to learn typewriting and shorthand somehow, and then I shall be a clerk."

"Clerk indeed!" cried Mrs. Creddle, losing her temper. "And what does that lead to, I should like to know? No girl clerk earns enough to buy food and lodging such as you would get at Miss Wilson's. I don't understand where the charm comes in, I'm sure, unless you want to be considered a lady. But you aren't one—and you'll never be one—though you do go out every morning and come back at night, and have a leather bag and a powdered nose instead of a cap and apron."

"Then I can tell you," said Caroline, pale and bright-eyed. "The charm is freedom. I'd starve before I'd ask permission to go to the pillar-box, and spend my nights in that old kitchen by myself."

"You know perfectly well that Miss Ethel would let you go out nearly every night," ejaculated Mrs. Creddle. "You're talking just for the sake of talking." Then she suddenly began to cry. "I can't bear for one of mine to behave like that—and I've always looked on you as my own child," she said, whimpering through a corner of her apron. "I've been poor all my life, but my word's been my bond. I never behaved shabby nor dishonourable to anybody that I knows on."

"I'm sorry, Aunt," said Caroline, flushing with distressful impatience. "But you have to think of yourself in these days, or get left. It's the rule all over the world now. And if everybody did the same, we should be all all right. Don't you see?"

Mrs. Creddle shook her head. "It might work out all right if the pushing-est sort was always the best," she said. Then, after a pause, she added, turning back towards the stairs: "Well, you may go and tell them yourself. I can't!"

"I don't want you to. I'm not afraid of those two old ladies," said Caroline, "if you are. So long!"

But as she went down the terrace again, it was not her own brilliant future which she saw before her mind's eye, but the desponding curve of Mrs. Creddle's figure going upstairs again to finish the bedrooms. Steadfastness, patience, endurance—without being actually aware of it, she saw those things embodied in that middle-aged woman's figure. Then her own spirit revolted from the suggestion. "Aunt doesn't understand," she said, half aloud. "You *have* to think of yourself first in these days."

Such was her mood as she emerged from Emerald Avenue into the main road, walked past the long field where the square board caught the eye at once amid all that springing verdure, and entered the garden of the Cottage. Immediately afterwards the front door opened and Miss Ethel stepped briskly forth. "Oh, there you are, Caroline. I am very pleased to see you. I suppose Willis will be bringing your box shortly, but in the meantime——"

"I aren't coming. I have only come to say I aren't coming," interrupted Caroline—the measure of her disturbance shown by the fact that she did not correct this lapse into the Holderness dialect. "I'm applying to be ticket collector on the promenade," she added, with a sort of defiant rudeness in her tone. She sub-consciously wanted Miss Ethel to be "horrid," feeling that it would make the situation easier to carry off with satisfaction to herself.

But Miss Ethel had been working since half-past six at unaccustomed blacking of the kitchen stove and such-like tasks in order that the new maid should see how things ought to be kept and maintain the same high standard, and she was too utterly weary and disappointed now, to do anything but reply with a very slight trembling of the lip: "I think you might have let me know before this, Caroline." For she felt that if she let herself go, she might burst into ignoble, undignified tears before this impertinent child—she, who never "gave way" even at a wedding or a funeral.

Caroline's quick eyes, however, had caught that passing quiver of the lips, and for one moment all her dreams of independence trembled in the balance. She was feeling—deeply as even Mrs. Creddle could wish—that she was behaving badly. Then Miss Ethel chanced to notice Caroline's blouse, which was made from her own summer dress of twenty years ago, and an irrepressible wave of hurt exasperation swept over her, rousing her to active resentment. "I must say I think you are treating me abominably, Caroline. Surely your Aunt Creddle is not a party to this?" she said in her sharpest tone. And though she would not have mentioned the blouse or any other benefit bestowed for the world, some thought of it must have rushed along the taut wires between her own mind and Caroline's, for the girl instantly flushed crimson and became defiant again. So the wavering balance crashed down on the side of the job on the promenade. Her whole future course, indeed, was decided in that instant, just by a look and a tone—though neither was aware of what had happened.

"Aunt had no idea I was trying for the place on the prom. until this morning," said Caroline quietly. "She's very upset about it, and tried her best to make me come to live with you after all, only I wouldn't. Nobody can blame her."

Miss Ethel opened her lips to administer a rebuke; then she felt it was no good and stood looking drearily in front of her. In so doing, her glance fell on the square board over the privet hedge, and that seemed somehow the visible sign of everything else that was happening in her life. Everything was changed. Without another word she turned back into the house, telling herself that it was of no use to fight against change; but at the bottom of her soul, she knew she *would* fight, so long as there was breath left in her.

"Stop a minute, Miss Ethel," said Caroline. "I am very sorry indeed I couldn't let you know before, and I have nothing against you or the place. It's only that I don't want to be a servant at all. Everybody must do the best they can for themselves in these days."

"I understand that you are like the rest of them. You want to go gadding about every night, no doubt," said Miss Ethel.

"And if I do?" said Caroline. "Where's the harm in it? Of course I want my freedom, Miss Ethel. We all do. That's why there aren't any servants to be had. You're free yourself and always have been. That's why you don't understand."

Miss Ethel felt a groping thought in the back of her mind. She—free! The long chain seemed to rattle through the empty years since childhood as she paused, though she thought she only heard the wind in the branches. "Oh, well; I suppose it is no use my saying any more. I trust for Mrs. Creddle's sake that you may be successful in your new employment. Good morning."

But in going over the threshold she swayed a little, because she had one of her bilious headaches and had eaten nothing since rising. Those headaches had been a feature of the establishment ever since Caroline would remember, and she recalled "Aunt Ellen" arraying a spotless tray in the kitchen while she herself sat eating gingerbread by the table. So all the kindnesses she had experienced in that house came back to war with this new spirit of prickly independence, and as she was fundamentally good-natured, she felt impelled to say impulsively: "Miss Ethel, I'll tell you what I could do. I might sleep here for a week or two and light the fire, and get breakfast ready and do any odd jobs for you. I should have time for that before I went out. One fortnight in the month I should only act as supply during meal hours—and that will leave me a lot of time during the day. I'll be glad to come and do that for my board and lodging, if you like: I'm not a big eater. Only I must have my nights free and no fixed time for getting in, of course."

Miss Ethel put her hand to her swimming head. Even in this extremity she could hardly bring herself to consider such a proposal. But the thought of washing up those greasy dishes after lunch was so intolerable that everything else faded into the background, and she had to humiliate herself for the sake of necessity. "Very well," she said faintly. "I shall be glad to accept your offer for the time being. We will talk about the remuneration later, but I think you can trust Mrs. Bradford and myself not to treat you unfairly."

"I'm not afraid of that," said Caroline, half ashamed: still she had to have it clear about her freedom. "You do understand about the evenings, though? Because I may want to go with Wilf—he's my friend, you know—to one of those dances on the prom., and then I shouldn't be back until after twelve."

"Yes, I understand," said Miss Ethel. "I'm much obliged to you," she forced herself to add, trying to rise above the dizziness which made her unable to think clearly.

"Then I'll be off and see if I can catch Willis with my box," said Caroline, hurrying away down the path.

Miss Ethel watched her go, wondering in a heavy sort of way if the girl would come back. It would not be in the least surprising if she failed to do so. Well, you could only take things as they came. Nothing was as it used to be. You couldn't calculate at all on what would happen in this strange new world....

Caroline, hastening down the road, had the same thought; but to her it brought a glorious sense of fresh vistas opening, of splendid conflicts in which she and her sort were bound to be victorious—she saw already a sun rising which would really warm rich and poor alike, and would make every one in the end happy and good.

No wonder Mr. Willis smiled at her when she went flying after him once more, all wind-blown hair and eyes a-shine; but he pulled up with a pretence of grumpiness, saying over his shoulder: "Well, what is it now? Have you rued throwing up your place?"

"No; I'm only going to help them a bit until they get a girl. You can't help being sorry for Miss Ethel."

"I'm to take your box on to the Cottage after all, then?" he said in a teasing way. "Well, well, it's a queer thing how women like to change their minds. I expect they're made so."

"I'm not," said Caroline. "I knew my own mind right enough: only I couldn't leave Miss Ethel with one of her bad headaches and nobody to do a thing for her. You'd be the first to blame me."

But he had whipped up his horse before she finished her sentence, and was already rattling away in the direction of the Cottage.

Chapter III
The Promenade

Pale blue sky with scudding clouds—a dun sea dappled with pale silver—and that intense greyish-white light on promenade, bleak-fronted houses and sparsely scattered visitors, which always makes everything so distinct as to seem unreal on such a day in Thorhaven—like an old copper-print.

As Caroline sat in her pay-box at the gate of the promenade, she had plenty of time to note these atmospheric conditions, but she only felt them. That grey, clear, windy brightness was mingled for all the rest of her life with what was to happen during the months between this morning and the end of September, when the job would be over. But now she was entirely immersed in her ticket issuing, when there was any to do, and in feeling excited and self-conscious and important when there was not. Book, pencil, pile of tickets were all meticulously ready, and she would not put her window down for a moment despite the north-east wind which swept round the little shelter.

But so early in the season there was scarcely a person to be seen about on the broad, grey stretch of the promenade, and the gardener's back as he worked hard at bedding out plants, looked in some way as if it still belonged to the easy-shirt-sleeved winter time, when Thorhaven was not expecting visitors. At last a little brisk woman with a neat figure came up to the turnstile, and Caroline greeted her with just that surprising warmth shown to casual acquaintances by stall-holders at a bazaar. "A season-ticket? Certainly. A pity not to get all the good out of it you can. Some people silly enough to wait until the season is half over and then pay just the same——" But the woman appreciated this cordiality at its true worth and was unresponsive. "So you've got the job. They'd be sorry to part with Maggie." Then pursing her lips, she placed her season ticket in her purse, and said with condescending asperity: "I want to go through, please."

So Caroline, thus reminded, hastily released the turnstile with her knee from within, and felt momentarily abashed. After a while, however, a solitary visitor approached the little window, and she was doubly brisk and official to make up for it.

"Day-ticket? But are you staying a week? If so, you'll find it much more to your advantage——" Until the visitor, who did not really want a weekly ticket at all, but happened to be of that ever-growing class which is cowed at once by any sign of bureaucratic authority, did as Caroline suggested.

But little by little this first eagerness wore off, and by the time she returned from the tea interval—during which her place had been taken by the girl who acted as "supply"—she had already begun to show faint beginnings of the slightly contemptuous, detached air of the official. She was pleasant still, but as a favour, and with the whole power of the Thorhaven Council at her back "Three in family, I think? I suppose you take one for Mildred?" And she expected Mrs. Creddle's neighbour to feel a little flattered by her remembering the size of the family.

But though justly irritated by that "Three in family, I think"—when Caroline had pulled pigtails with Mildred only yesterday, as it were—the good woman was actually pleased when Caroline "held up" a stout person in a fur coat and a motor veil to add pleasantly: "I suppose you are expecting visitors this week?" Which remark is the recognized conversational small change in Thorhaven, during spring and summer, scarcely more personal than the "Fine day!" of the country labourers who live in the still untouched country beyond the Cottage.

But if Mrs. Creddle's neighbour said to herself that Caroline would soon be too big for her boots, there remained a slight glow of satisfaction in being acknowledged as an old acquaintance while an affluent person from a car was kept waiting. It is therefore not surprising that Wilfred Ball felt the same glow greatly intensified when he strolled up to the pay-box, twirling his walking-stick, to take his stand near by as the future proprietor of the girl inside. Perhaps the young husband of a great prima donna may feel nearly as sophisticated and proud and "in it" when he strolls carelessly into the dressing-room where the bouquets of admirers overflow upon the floor—but this is scarcely likely, for he would not have the morning freshness still on him of a life spent so far between Thorhaven and Flodmouth.

Every now and then he took a little walk up and down the promenade, either alone or with a casual acquaintance, but he soon returned to enjoy close at hand this epoch-making evening. For now, he felt, there was nothing that could keep the Wilfred Balls back from those pinnacles of affluence which a combination of the more easily assimilated comic papers and articles on Self-Help had enabled him to envisage: Self-Help kind showing how a poor man might grow rich, and the comic papers how he might spend his money when he got it.

As the wife of a wealthy man, Caroline would be All Right. He had had his doubts before, at times, because he really felt it was a come-down for a young fellow in a seed-merchant's office to be engaged to a servant. And remorse had something to do now with his ardour, because he really had begun to wonder if he could "keep on" with it, when Caroline was a true servant, living in, like the little maids all up and down the new streets. He had seen himself standing at a corner waiting for her under a lamp-post on her nights out, and had found his faithfulness wavering.

Still, she was Caroline—and they had "gone together" ever since the time when he first perceived that a "girl" was as necessary to man's estate as a dressy lounge suit and a Homburg hat. He did not like to behave badly to her. And now he had been rewarded. He had achieved the difficult feat mentioned in those articles he so casually read in the train, of keeping one eye on the main chance and the other on the example of Sir Galahad. Now he was still engaged to somebody who took tickets on the prom. and was a young lady—and was yet Caroline. No wonder he stood and beamed, and walked away and twirled his stick and cocked his hat, and then came back and beamed again.

Other youths of her acquaintance, or enterprising strangers going through the barrier, had to content themselves with a "Good evening, miss," or at most some more or less dashing remark about the weather; but *he* was the one to help her on with her coat when the brilliant shades of blue and yellow on the sentry-box had faded into grey: it was *his* privilege to walk her off with a hand through her arm, feeling sure that the three elderly spinsters and the one middle-aged gentleman who chanced to be about just there wondered who that gay dog was, and thought him no end of a fellow.

"Well, Carrie, how did you like it?" he said as they went along.

"Oh, it was all right," said Caroline in an off-handed fashion—but she also had an elated consciousness of being important, and did not care a bit though her feet were stone-cold from sitting still in the sentry-box.

So talking eagerly, they went down the main road until the last avenue was left behind and the loneliness of stars and sea-wind fronted them. Only one light glimmered above the privet hedge from an upper room in the Cottage.

At the gate they stopped to kiss and say good night as usual, but the excitement of a new experience had stirred Caroline's emotions, and Wilf's pride in her had also roused the possessive instinct in him, so that the kiss they exchanged was a little different from the almost passionless salute to which they had long grown accustomed. Wilf's eyes shone and Caroline's cheeks were flushed when they drew back from each other. She began to speak quickly, nervously. "Well, so long! They'll think I'm never coming."

"Here! Hold on a minute." He caught her round the waist. "I say, Carrie, it's rotten you having to go in, and me stopping outside. I wish you'd never promised to."

"It wouldn't have made any difference if I had been staying at Uncle Creddle's. They wouldn't want company at this time of night," she answered, peering up at him uneasily through the starry twilight.

"Carrie!" He held her closer, his thin, boyish arms trembling a little. "I wish to goodness we could have a home of our own. There's some houses going to be built in that field there. I wish we could apply for one of them."

"Well, we can't," said Caroline, touched by some wistful tone in the lad's voice to a deeper tenderness for him than she had hitherto known. "We have nothing to get married on. People would only laugh at us."

"But you wish it, same as me, Carrie? If I was one of them rich young chaps that can plank down the money for a half-year's rent and a mahog'ny suite, like I do for a packet of cigs., you'd be ready to get married, Carrie?"

It was the first time they had seriously talked of marriage, though they had been "going together" ever since Caroline knew that a 'boy' was as essential to her grown-up panoply as hairpins, and she felt something indefinable at the back of her mind which was not pleasure; and yet it was not fear—— She turned from her own emotions with a sort of relief. "Goodness! There's the church clock striking a quarter to eleven. We must have been three-quarters of an hour coming from the prom. here. I know Miss Ethel goes to bed at ten, and she'll have been sitting up for me."

"Never mind. You're only stopping to oblige. They ought to be jolly thankful to you, whatever time you turn up," babbled Wilf—all impatient excitement. "Carrie, just one more. I must——"

He clung to her, then let her go. She ran up the path towards the house while he stood there, listening to her footsteps and yet restraining himself from following her, as a matter of course. For the idea of running after her and holding her in his arms by force, as he wanted to do, simply never entered his mind. Despite that dark lane and the evening hour, the chivalry of the ordinary decent Anglo-Saxon man—which some races are unable to understand—stood like a sentinel at the door of his desires.

Caroline entered the door of the Cottage in a state of hurry and excitement; but the empty kitchen seemed to act on it like a sort of emotional cold douche. The varnished walls, the neatly set chairs, the clock ticking so loudly above the mantel-shelf, all seemed somehow unnatural, with the unnaturalness of empty houses where steps go echoing— echoing—though nobody is there.

She hastily put the kettle on the gas-ring, then prepared a glass for Miss Ethel's hot water and two cups for Mrs. Bradford's cocoa and her own. But as the water would not boil all at once she stood there watching the little blue and yellowish flames of that unsatisfactory Thorhaven gas splutter under the kettle. All sorts of thoughts went scurrying about her mind as the clock measured the seconds—tick-tock! tick-tock!—over her head.

How silly of Wilf to begin to talk about marrying at all. But, of course, if you were engaged—only she and Wilf weren't engaged. They'd been "going together," of course, but she had no ring. She had never considered herself really engaged. Neither had Aunt Creddle——

But the kettle suddenly boiled over, so she filled the glass and the cups, and hurried off with the tray, her head still so full of her own engrossing thoughts that she did not become aware that visitors were present until she was well inside the room.

"Oh, Caroline, you can just put the tray down on the round table," said Miss Ethel, high and cool. It was plain that she thought the hour very late, and that Caroline's red cheeks, disordered hair and hat rakishly on one side did not please her.

Caroline's face became still more flushed and she flung up her head as she crossed the room, then put down the tray with a considerable clatter. But the clatter was unintentional—though Miss Ethel would not have believed this—and was due to a small piece of needlework on the table which caused the cup and glass to stand unevenly on the tray. Caroline heard the sharp indrawing of Miss Ethel's breath on the way to the door, and her whole being was in a prickly heat of defiance and embarrassment— "Only wait until to-morrow morning! To-morrow morning, they would just hear about it. They might look somewhere else for a girl who would let herself be spoken to as if she was something unpleasant that crawled——"

But through the fiery mist that seemed to blind her as she re-crossed the room, she heard another voice speaking: "Good evening, Miss Raby. How did you like your first day at the promenade?"

It was a lovely voice, clear yet mellow, and Caroline, despite all her anger and wounded pride, felt obliged to answer civilly: "Oh, I liked it all right, Miss Temple, thank you."

The door closed; there was a pause while Caroline's high heels clacked faintly across the tiled floor of the hall, and then a sound burst forth like the sudden chattering of rooks when they are startled in their nests by a shot fired close at hand.

"Well, I never! Coming in at a quarter to eleven and taking that attitude!" said Mrs. Bradford, in her heavy wheezy contralto.

"It's the same in everything. The world's upside down," jerked out Miss Ethel, flushed and tight-lipped. "Oh, we little knew what a lovely world we lived in twenty years ago. We took it all for granted. Good servants: low prices. People knowing their duty."

"Did they, though?" said Laura Temple. "I think it must have been perfectly horrid to be a maid-servant in those days. Only out one night a week, and once on Sunday at most, and kept as close during the rest of the time as if you were in a nunnery."

"They were happy, though," said Miss Ethel. "Happier, I think, than these girls are now. Look at Ellen! Wasn't she the picture of content?"

Then Mrs. Graham's high voice shrilled across the buzz of talk. "Mine actually wears silk stockings on her evenings out—silk stockings!"

"What I say," boomed Mr. Graham soothingly, "best make up your minds to let things go. You can't alter them. My wife here worked herself up into such a state of nerves during the war that she had to take bromide for months, and I'm not going to let that happen again. I don't allow any discussion of national difficulties, either at home or abroad. We read the head-lines in the newspaper so that we know what has actually happened, and we leave other people's speculations about things alone. Only way to go on living with any comfort."

Mrs. Graham looked across at her husband with affection, and murmured aside to Laura Temple: "It is really on Arthur's account that we have banned discussion on strikes and Ireland and so on. He gets indigestion if he dwells on painful topics. So I just make things as comfortable as I can in our own house, and let the world take care of itself. A wife's first duty is to make her husband happy, as you will find out before long, my dear."

Laura smiled back at Mrs. Graham, with the colour deepening a shade under the soft brown eyes which exactly matched her voice.

"There's no idea of our being married yet, Mrs. Graham," she said. "For one thing, our house will not be ready for some time." But behind her quiet words she was saying to herself that never, never would she and Godfrey emulate Mr. and Mrs. Graham's system of guarding the common existence from anything found disturbing to comfort, with a tame good conscience ready to call it conjugal devotion.

"I expected to see Mr. Wilson with you to-night," murmured Mrs. Graham: then she leaned nearer to Laura and said in a still lower tone: "I suppose he is in disgrace here for being the agent for the sale of that field beyond the privet hedge?"

"Yes. They think he might somehow have avoided selling it because he is a connection of theirs," replied Laura. "But the Warringborns would only have taken their business to another firm, of course. Godfrey says a man must look after himself in these days. You can't afford to offend a valuable client for the sake of a second cousin."

"Ridiculous!" said Mrs. Graham. Then she paused a moment until her husband's voice again made confidences possible. "Oh, they will get used to the idea of houses being built there in time. Look how disturbed they were about Emerald Avenue when it was first started."

"Yes." Laura paused, her charming, irregular face with its creamy complexion and frame of brown wavy hair turned to the speaker, and her broad forehead wrinkled a little, as it was when she was puzzled or perturbed. "But I really am sorry for them now. You see, the privet hedge hid all those streets from the garden. They could forget there were any there. Now they won't be able to forget." She paused. "I simply daren't tell them who has bought Thorhaven Hall. I know it gave even me a shock, because I always used to feel an awed sensation—the sort you have going into a strange church or a museum when you are little—whenever I called at the Hall. It was so dark and big and quiet, and the old butler took your name as if you were at a funeral, and ought to be awfully honoured to have been asked to attend. I simply can't imagine the Perritt's there."

Mrs. Graham rose. "Oh, I believe the Perritt children are very sweet. And there is something rather nice about Mrs. Perritt, I'm told."

Miss Ethel looked across the room, and it was evident that she heard the last remark, for she said in a dry tone: "Lots of people would discover something sweet about me if I came into ten thousand a year; nothing like money for enabling the eye to detect hidden charms."

Mrs. Graham laughed somewhat uneasily. "How amusing you are, Miss Ethel! I often tell Arthur it is quite refreshing to have a chat with you." But for all that, she began to move towards the door.

Laura also rose, and it could be now seen that her tall figure was a trifle angular and immature, and must remain so, for she was already twenty-eight years old. "I will come as far as your house, Mrs. Graham," she said. "Godfrey promised to call for me there."

"Well! No good crying over spilt milk," said Mr. Graham, standing and shaking down his trousers—after a habit he had—with his hands in his pockets. "Things will never be the same again in our day, Miss Ethel."

"No." Mrs. Bradford, who had been silent, as she often was, unexpectedly entered the conversation, saying in her heavy voice: "Things will never be the same again." And a brief silence followed her words. You could fancy them echoing in every heart there.

"I remember getting oranges twelve a penny in Flodmouth," continued Mrs. Bradford, stirred to unwonted intellectual effort. "Twelve a penny! Perhaps you don't believe me, but I did."

No one taking up the gage which Mrs. Bradford thus threw down, the guests said farewell and then went out into the starlight.

As they walked along, all Laura's thoughts were about the lover waiting for her; but Mr. and Mrs. Graham could not get rid of that slight sense of inward discomfort—stirred afresh by Mrs. Bradford's first remark—which many middle-aged people experience as a result of Fate's ruthlessly quick forcing of new wine into old bottles.

As they passed the new streets there was an odd light here and there in the shadowy rows of houses, and when they turned the corner the sea-wind was full in their faces. The glass roof of the Promenade Hall glimmered faintly under the immense sweep of starlit sky, and the quiet waves drew away—"C-raunch! C-r-raunch!"—from the piece of gravelled shore which the tide had reached. The good-sized, semi-detached houses built in a row opposite the promenade stood all so black and lifeless that Mr. Graham's click of the iron gate sounded quite roistering on the still night. Then the front door opened and light streamed out, illuminating the figure of a man of medium height, rather stockily built, who came quickly down the little path, calling out as he approached: "I'd almost given you up, Laura. I should have fetched you from the Cottage, only I thought the old girls would cut up rough. I suppose they haven't forgiven me for that notice board yet? They think I'm a low fellow, I know."

"No, no," said Laura, smiling. "A man with the Wilson blood in his veins couldn't be really low, Godfrey—only misguided. You know they think even a bad Wilson must after all be slightly better at the bottom than other people."

"Jolly good theory," he said, throwing out his broad chest and laughing down at his lady, who had slipped her hand through his arm. "I hope they converted you."

Then they all laughed—though there was nothing at all amusing in his remark—simply because he was so sure of himself and seemed to expect it, Laura glanced up at his large-featured face with soft brown eyes full of admiring affection, and the scar on his cheek from a shrapnel wound still had power to move her. For he had "done splendidly" in the war, enlisting in 1915 and showing marked courage, though his very highly-developed instinct for self-preservation had enabled him to escape dangers where some men might have been caught. No wonder that as Laura stood there with her hand through his strong arm, she thrilled to the certainty that he would break with ease through every obstacle in life, both for himself and her.

"I'm sorry to have kept you so long," she said. "But I think we have fixed up everything about the Fête for the Women's Convalescent Home now. We are so short of funds that we must do something."

"Yes," said Mr. Graham, "the people who used to support it haven't the money to give any longer; and those who have it, won't give, I suppose."

"Oh, don't let us start that all over again," said Mrs. Graham. "Arthur, you will take cold standing here in the night air. Laura, won't you come in for a few minutes?"

But Laura had no desire to share that cosy half-hour by the fire during which Mr. Graham would press his Lizzie to pile on coal and put more sugar in her cocoa for the good of her health, and she would press him to take a little whisky and hot water—in spite of the high price—for the same reason.

Chapter IV
The Three Men

Miss Ethel glanced out of the bedroom window next morning as she was opening it more widely, and suddenly, as she looked, every muscle stiffened. What were those three men doing a few yards beyond the privet hedge? But her reason refused to let in the thought that followed. It was preposterous to imagine they would start building there first, with all the field to choose from. Besides, she had never heard of the land being sold— the board was still in its place. Of course, if the land had been sold, the board would have been removed.

She knelt down to say her prayers, beginning with the very same which she used to repeat when she was a little girl by her mother's knee: only the numbers of near relatives then mentioned by name had since dwindled, one by one, as they passed over that bridge from life to eternal life. Then "Our Father"—but the thought of the three men came in between, and she found herself saying "Amen" without having prayed at all. Then she started over again. "Thy kingdom come." But her mind shot away at once from that image of divine order to the unrest by which she was troubled. Pictures of strikes—staring headlines—these crowded in upon her as she knelt, and she rose from her knees still without having really prayed to God.

Then she came downstairs to breakfast to find that Caroline had cleaned the room and had set the breakfast with a certain daintiness, while leaving dust thick on the corners of the floor and under the clock on the mantel-piece. Still, it was such a relief not to have to get up and prepare the breakfast and light the fire that Miss Ethel tried to forget the dust. Of course, after Caroline had gone out, she could go round with a brush and duster, but it was a great rest in the meantime not to start the day with tasks too arduous for her strength and her unaccustomed muscles.

Mrs. Bradford, however, who never felt able to help in the house-work herself, owing to something obscure about the legs, would persist in talking all breakfast time about the dust and Caroline's other shortcomings. "Never know when you have her. This week she is eating at all sorts of hours because she has to go to the promenade and free the other girl at meal times; then next week she will be here at meals only. It is your affair, Ethel. When I came back I let you go on doing the housekeeping, though I am a married woman. But I know when I had a house to manage myself, I should never have put up with such goings-on."

"It's all very well to talk. Neither should I, five years ago," retorted Miss Ethel. "In fact, I should not do so now if there were any alternative. But you know perfectly well that we could not afford to keep a good maid at the present rate of wages, even if we could get one."

Mrs. Bradford contented herself with peering irritatingly through her spectacles at the dusty places after that, because Miss Ethel's statement admitted of no argument; for Mr. Bradford left his widow the honour and glory of the conjugal state and practically nothing more tangible. But to Miss Ethel's generation the mere fact of being married meant more than the present one can understand, and she was accustomed to acquiesce in her sister's air of heavy superiority, though she knew herself to be much the more intelligent of the two.

Still her temper felt so rasped as she went out into the kitchen carrying a tray of crockery that she was in no mood to receive kindly any more new suggestions made to her, and when Caroline asked for a latch-key as a matter of course, she replied stiffly: "I'm sorry, but I could not think of such a thing, Caroline. I must say I rather wonder at your asking it. Your aunt Ellen——"

"Aunt Ellen lived in different times," said Caroline, flushing and throwing up her head. "I am going to a dance with my boy at the Promenade Hall, and it doesn't finish till twelve. I didn't want you to sit up so late for me, that was all."

Miss Ethel also flushed a little on her thin cheekbones, while the left side of her face twitched a little as it did when she was agitated; but that was all the sign she gave of the tumult of irritation, impatience and hurt pride which surged within her. That Ellen's niece should dare to speak to her like that! Still, she knew that she was worn out and could not go on doing all the work of the house, and they would never get anyone else to help them who would be as cheap and respectable as Caroline; so she must put up with it. By a great effort, she managed to control her temper and to say, almost agreeably: "Does Mrs. Creddle know you are going to this dance with a young man?"

"Of course she does," said Caroline, still rather defiant. "I'm not ashamed of it. There's nothing between me and Wilf that I should want to hide from Aunt Creddle."

For without knowing it, Miss Ethel had touched upon a delicate point which Caroline was far more sensitive about than Laura—for instance— would have been; because girls of Caroline's sort have to guard their chastity themselves, while those like Laura are careless, because it has always been guarded for them by somebody else. Still Miss Ethel saw that

Caroline was offended, so added after a pause: "If Mrs. Creddle approves of your going, of course it is not my affair. But you must see for yourself that I could not let a girl under my roof stay out until midnight without asking the question. That would be fair neither to you nor to myself."

"No," muttered Caroline. "I didn't mean anything either. Only it has been such a—a rotten thing in the past for every one to think that servant girls must be misbehaving themselves if they stopped out after half-past ten."

"They often were," said Miss Ethel grimly. "Because if they weren't, they remembered it was time to come in and came. But here is your latch-key." And she went out of the kitchen, not daring to trust herself to say any more for fear she should offend Caroline and be left without any help in the house.

But she suffered an almost physical ache from the readjustment of her behaviour to the changed conditions of life as she went upstairs to her bedroom. It was constantly happening like that—there was no time for the irritation to subside before something roused it again. And Miss Ethel took no comfort from the fact that all over the world people were more or less suffering in the same way, because she only vaguely realized that this was so.

She knew, however, that she felt humiliated as she handed over the latch-key to Caroline, contrary to all her own principles, just before the girl went out to collect tickets on the promenade during the dinner interval.

The morning was cold for the first week in June, but a brief spell of August weather in May had acted as a bait to the visitors that Thorhaven lived on now, just as it used to live on the crabs and mackerel and codling and shrimps caught in the bay. But that time was so entirely over and done with that there were not enough real fishermen left to man the lifeboat, and the smell of fish and brine had departed, even from the narrow alleys in the old part of the town where it had been for hundreds of years. Now the owners of the smallest and most inconvenient cottages hung clean curtains, put "To Let, Furnished" bills in the windows, and went off to camp in booths, tents, out-houses or in any place where they could find shelter.

So this morning, though it was still so early in the year, provident mothers with little children, and others bent on a cheaper holiday than August could afford, were walking in light dresses about the roads, emerging gaily from little front gates, clustering round the little bright shops with their piles of fruit and cakes and sweets. It was a bright-coloured company that Caroline saw about the streets as she went along the road towards the familiar row of yellowish-red houses where the Creddles lived.

Mrs. Creddle was ironing, and she looked up from the board almost in tears as her niece entered the kitchen. "Oh, Carrie," she began at once, "I thought you'd be coming. I am in such a way. I don't know whatever you'll say to me, but I've burnt a great place on the front width of your dress. I was pressing it out, because you'd got it all crumpled up in your drawer upstairs, and then Winnie tumbled down on the fender and made her nose bleed. You never saw such a sight. So somehow in my fluster I left the iron on the dress. I can't think how I ever came to do such a thing."

Caroline looked from the burnt front breadth to Mrs. Creddle's agitated face and said nothing. Her disappointment was so great that she must have "told Aunt Creddle off" if she had opened her lips, and she did not want to do that, because she could see the poor woman was distressed enough already.

"Oh, well; never fret!" she managed to say at last. "Plenty more dances before I'm dead. We won't make a trouble about this one."

"But I do," said Mrs. Creddle, dissolving into tears at this kindly address. "Me—that always wants you to enjoy yourself while you can—to have gone and spoilt your only party dress! I could hit myself, I could, if it would do any good."

Upon this little Winnie, still tearful from past sorrows, began to cry loudly again. "You shan't hit yourself, Mummy. I won't let you hit yourself."

"Here!" said Caroline, putting a parcel down on the table. "I got some kippers as I came past the fish shop. I know Uncle Creddle fancies one with his tea."

"You shouldn't have done that, Carrie," said Mrs. Creddle, wiping her eyes. "Kippers is dear nowadays, and I'm sure you have plenty to do with your money."

"Nonsense!" said Caroline. "I'm rolling in riches. You see my keep costs me nothing, and I have all I earn to spend." She went towards the door, saying over her shoulder: "Now, don't you worry about the dress. I can easily get another, and you may cut this up into a Sunday frock for Winnie."

"That I never shall——" began Mrs. Creddle: then her round face became suddenly illuminated. "Why, yes, so I will. And then you can have the one Miss Temple gave me to make into something for the children. It's a queer sort of colour—neither red nor yellow—but it looks all right by night. She said Mr. Wilson didn't like to see her in it. Of course, she's bigger than you, but they wear things so short and loose nowadays that I dare say if I hem the bottom up it will be all right. My word, I am glad I thought of it. I hate keeping you away from the dance."

Caroline paused on the threshold. "I don't like wearing other people's clothes," she said doubtfully.

"No; but Miss Temple's different. She gives things with such a good heart and she never talks about what she does. I can't see that you need mind her," urged Mrs. Creddle. "There's no time to get another dress. It's that, or stopping away from the dance."

Still Caroline hesitated, standing there on the blue linoleum with the bright light shining through the open door on her face. "Oh! all right," she exclaimed finally, then glanced at the clock. "Goodness, I shall be late! You can measure the dress against my old frock. I haven't a minute." And she was out, banging the door behind her.

But before she was many yards away, the door burst open again and Mrs. Creddle's anxious face looked out. "Carrie! Carrie! You don't want to tell your uncle if you come across him. He'd have a fit if he knew you were going to the dance on the prom., let alone wearing that fine frock. You know what he is!"

"Don't I just!" responded Caroline, her spirits beginning to rise again. "Well, what he doesn't know he can't grieve about, so you keep a still tongue in your head and I'll run round for the dress when I leave the prom. after tea." Then at last she was running along the grey pavements with the clean wind blowing towards her from the sea.

In her haste she almost ran into three men who were coming along from the direction of the Cottage with measuring tapes and other appliances in their hands, but she took no particular notice of them, never dreaming that these three commonplace looking men in ordinary dark clothes could even now be haunting another person's imagination with the sinister effect of birds of prey who mark the approach of an invading horde.

But Miss Ethel had seen them from her upper window, and the sight of them walking about in the field had produced an acute physical feeling of nausea and faintness; for her fear lest the field should be built upon and the last seclusion spoilt, had already made one of those deep ruts in the mind along which every thought runs when not actually driven in another direction. And each time Miss Ethel's thoughts passed that way, the rut was bound to become deeper. Though she imagined herself so self-controlled, and seemed so safe as she went quietly about her work removing the dust from corners where Caroline had left it, she was indeed a woman in real danger, still fighting all the great forces of change arrayed against her, and which she must give in to or be destroyed.

Chapter V
The Dance on the Promenade

A night in June brings to the mind of most people soft airs—the scent of roses—a time when the young can sit out-of-doors in the moonlight, and the middle-aged may venture forth without risk of catching cold. But even on such a night in Thorhaven there is a nipping freshness at sunset which keeps the mind alert instead of lulling the senses—giving an exquisite clearness to the thoughts of lovers: at any rate, to the thoughts of lovers like Laura Temple.

But visitors did not realize this, only remarking to each other with disapproval that it was much colder than in Flodmouth, and that you always needed a thick coat in the evening at Thorhaven, whatever the time of year. At the present moment, however, most of them were hurrying away from the wide expanse of shore and sea that glimmered under the reflection of the sunset, for dancing was to start at half-past eight in the glass hall which filled the centre of the promenade.

The girl in charge of the pay-box was busier than usual, and Caroline stood at a little distance taking a professional interest in the number of tickets sold. Her first feeling of importance had worn off, but she had the correct official air of detachment, glancing at the throng which hurried through the barrier with a sort of indulgent superiority, while the band under the glass roof of the hall tootled faintly against the deep roll of the waves. The immensity of the arched sky above, with the dim, flat land on one side, and the expanse of darkening sea on the other, seemed to give to those dance tunes an indescribable melancholy. They seemed to epitomize all the shortness and futility of the little lives which had flickered for a few years on the edge of that sea and then gone out.

Not that Caroline thought of this, being a normal, healthy girl, but a shadow of the thought fell across her bright path and she shivered slightly, drawing her coat closer round her throat. "Come on," she said, turning to Wilf, who stood near waiting for her. "That band gives me the pip, hearing it from the outside. You want something louder than that near the sea."

"Well, you had the steam roundabouts on Bank Holiday, and you didn't like that," said Wilf cheerfully. "Some folks are never satisfied."

"Look!" said Caroline. "There's that friend of Miss Laura Temple's."

Wilf turned to watch a group coming through the barrier. They were young people from some of the larger houses that had been built to accommodate business people from Flodmouth, but evidently not of the sort that desires constant gaiety, or they would not have lived in Thorhaven. Now they had made up a little party to come and dance in the promenade hall, with the simple object of enjoying a fair floor and a band that played in tune.

As they passed Wilf and Caroline, one said eagerly to the other: "Where's Laura Temple? I don't see anything of her. She and Godfrey Wilson were to have waited here for us."

"Oh, didn't you know? Got a sore throat and can't——"

They went on, and Caroline breathed again. She had never thought of Laura being at a dance on the promenade, and the sudden idea of meeting the original owner of the flame-coloured dress gave her a little shock. The whole situation, as it might have been, opened out in front of her for a moment or two, bristling with unpleasantnesses, and she glanced down at the edge of colour appearing under her coat with a distinct regret that she had been persuaded by Mrs. Creddle into wearing the dress. Better far to have stopped at home.

Then there was Wilf, taking her arm with cool possessiveness. "Come on, Carrie! *I* aren't going to stop here all night while you think over your sins." He laughed and the two girls standing near him laughed too—not that they felt amused, but because laughter was the accepted accompaniment to such conversations.

So they went along together under the first star that hung high in the green sky, and the Flamborough light trembled across the water just as they entered the hot and crowded hall. The spectators—mostly middle-aged— sat in a solid phalanx round the sides of the room doing knitting or crochet, hoping against hope to see other folks make fools of themselves, or afford a spectacle of some sort that might be worth watching.

Already several couples were whirling round on the polished floor, and Caroline, who had come bare-headed, took off her coat at once, placed it in a corner with Wilf's hat, and swung out into the dance. At first Wilf and she were only conscious of being looked at and anxious to do their steps with credit, but after a little while Wilf became agreeably conscious that people were interested in them. He held his partner more jauntily and redoubled his attention to the dance, occasionally whispering some sally into Caroline's ear to show how much at ease he was, and how dashingly he could "carry it off."

Caroline on her part now felt an exhilarated conviction that her own appearance in the flame-coloured dress was the source of attraction; and every time she passed a certain place where a dark screen hung behind the glass, she glanced at a revolving vision of excited eyes and glowing draperies.

The low rays of the sinking sun struck through the glass panes on the western side of the hall and mingled with the gas, which was already turned on, to create a sort of strange half-light in which nobody seemed quite real. The couples swam round and round in this peculiar radiance, while the heavy figures watching appeared to recede and grow more dense.

The music ceased and they stood still, breathing quickly, hemmed in by a large group of people. After a while Caroline suddenly felt a touch on her shoulder from behind. "I say, Laura, I thought you were not——" And she turned round sharply to see Wilson with outstretched arm peering between heads. "Oh," he exclaimed—"so sorry! I took you for Miss Temple. I only caught a glimpse of your dress."

"It's all right," said Caroline abruptly, crimson to the roots of her hair. Then the music started again and she seized hold of Wilf's arm. "Come along! We don't want to lose any of this."

Wilson was left behind among a group who were not dancing at the moment, but gradually they moved away and he stood there alone, steady on his feet—almost impressively self-reliant and sure of himself, though he was neither tall nor handsome. As he stood idly looking on, he began to notice the flame-coloured dress which had been Laura's flashing in and out of the more sober garments. It displayed a good deal of Caroline's figure, which was slim and clean made—something like a Tanagra statuette, but less curved. He found himself watching for her every time as she came round, and finally a thought darted across his mind—a nymph on fire. Why!—he chuckled softly to himself, pleased by the apt phrase and feeling clever—that was what it *was*, by gad! But where on earth had she got a gown exactly like the one which had suited Laura so badly?

When the music stopped he moved from his place and walked straight up to Caroline. "I must apologize for having touched you on the arm, but I only caught a glimpse of your dress through the crowd," he said, "and at first I thought you were Miss Temple. She has a dress exactly like the one you are wearing."

"Oh, it's all right," repeated Caroline, beginning to move off. Then she suddenly stopped short. After all, he would get to know. She was not going to look as if she were ashamed of what she had done. "It is the same dress," she said, throwing up her head with a jerk, as she did when she was defiant. "Miss Temple gave it to my aunt, Mrs. Creddle, and I'm wearing it because Aunt burnt a frock of mine."

"Lucky thing she did," said Wilson easily. "I can't quite see Mrs. Creddle in this gown—at least, if she is the lady I have encountered at Miss Wilson's."

"Ha! ha!" laughed Wilf, feeling he owed it to his own dignity to assert himself and join in somehow, but finding a difficulty in beginning.

"Miss Temple didn't mean it to be worn. It was to make best frocks for the little ones or something like that," said Caroline. "But I shan't wear it again, so they'll have the benefit of it all the same."

"Well, I'm sure the original wearer would be delighted if she could see you in it," said Wilson.

"Just what *I* say," put in Wilf, seizing his chance. "Never saw Carrie look better. She'll be immensely grateful to Miss Temple for the loan of it, of course. Wonderful how the ladies can come to the rescue of each other. Now, we men—it's a queer thing, Mr. Wilson, when you come to think of it, but I don't suppose there's two pairs of legs alike in this hall."

"No?" said Wilson interestedly. "Well, I believe you are right. It is strange what things can be discovered about life by keeping one's eyes open. I daresay you don't let much escape yours."

"Oh, I don't go about with them *shut*, of course," said Wilf modestly. "But I'm like that. It's no credit to me. Always was from a kid."

Wilson glanced round, letting his gaze pass over the little party from the new villas with whom he was fairly well acquainted, then he turned to Wilf. "I don't seem to see many people I know here. I wonder if you would mind my having a turn with Miss Creddle?" he said. "That is, if she does not object."

"My name isn't Creddle; it's Raby," said Caroline.

"Oh, I don't mind. I'll console myself somehow just for one dance," said Wilf grandly, for he was feeling greatly flattered—first by being regarded as Caroline's keeper, and also by the deferential attitude of this older man who had reached the place in life where he would like to be.

"Will you be so kind, Miss Raby?" said Wilson.

So Caroline, unable to refuse, allowed him to put his arm round her and guide her out into the moving throng. After the first moment or two when she was entirely engrossed in feeling annoyed with Wilf, she began to experience a most peculiar and yet agreeable sensation—as if she need not trouble about anything in the whole world ever any more. She remained aware of the music, of the many-coloured throng going round and round in the last rays of the sunset which mingled so strangely with the artificial light from the roof of the hall—still she seemed to be carried along apart from it all; to be enclosed by something which emanated from the man who held her, and which isolated them both. Once or twice he made some trivial remark, but nothing to need thinking about; and when the music stopped she felt for a second or two a sort of dizziness—like coming too suddenly out of a dim room into a bright sunlight.

"I must have met you somewhere before," he was saying. "I am sure I remember your face."

"Yes." She felt the odd dizziness leaving her. With an effort she forced herself to become alert and keen again. "I expect you've seen me collecting tickets. I and another girl take it in turns."

"Ah! That must be what I am thinking of," he said. But he searched his mind in vain for the recollection of a girl at that little window in the pay-box who could by any magic of clothes and swaying steps be transformed even for five minutes into a nymph on fire.

But Wilf came up and he had to let her go—felt, indeed, no particular desire to detain her; for Caroline greeted her admirer with such real relief that he had no doubt of her feelings. She just caught hold of Wilf's arm and began at once to move in time to the music, while that gratified young man nodded jauntily over her shoulder to Wilson and sailed off, thinking himself very grown-up and experienced and important—a man with a female for whom he was responsible—one of the initiate.

Almost immediately after that Wilson went away, but it was three hours later before Caroline and Wilf, having danced their fill, emerged into the coolness of the midnight air. As they walked down the dim promenade together, Wilf was still talking about Wilson. "Some chaps say he is so stand-offish, but I always hold that people treat you as you treat them. And if the fellows say anything of the sort to me in the train, to-morrow, I shall just tell them they're wrong. Most pleasant, he can be, when he likes."

"Why shouldn't he be?" said Caroline. "You're as good as he is."

"I know that, but I haven't got what he has. You don't understand the world yet, Carrie, my dear," he said largely. "I tell you, that man can smell when there's going to be land in the market, if there's anything to be made out of it. Sort of second smell. Ha! ha!"

Carrie laughed. "Go on! You really *are* a one, Wilf!" But her encouraging laughter was a veil to hide her thoughts—the old veil used a thousand thousand times since life and love began.

"Look here, Carrie," Wilf began again, suddenly serious. "What man has done, man can do. I didn't mean to tell you yet, but I will." He lowered his voice, glancing round at the calm immensity of the moonlight night lest any one should hear him. "If I go on as I am doing, I shall be worth five thousand pounds before I die."

Carrie clutched his arm, looking into the smooth, boyish face so near her own, with its young curves and sharpnesses made wistful by the moonlight. She did not know why, but was suddenly filled with a sort of aching, protective pity when she heard those words mingling with the sound of the sea. It was Wilf's youngness and littleness in the face of that immensity. "Five thousand pounds before I die!" And the sea beating on the shore just the same——

But out of it all, the only words she found were: "I know you will, Wilf. You'll do more than that. Look how your governor spoke about your shorthand last week."

"And that brings me," continued Wilf, growing more and more solemn and important, "to what I really want to say. I'm going to get the ring to-morrow, Carrie, so you'd better lend me that old one of your mother's you have on, for a measure. I aren't going to ask you what stones you'd like, because I shall get diamonds. A dress ring without diamonds is nothing, and I mean my wife to have the best."

"Diamonds! Oh, Wilf!" said Carrie. But the first glow of surprise and pleasure passed almost before it was there. "Wife!" She didn't want that. She wasn't ready for that. "Don't think of such a thing. We can't be married for years and years. Besides, I don't want a ring. It—it hasn't got so far, yet. We have always been friends, but when it comes to settling down together for life——"

He swung round. "What on earth do you mean?" he demanded. "Are you keeping a loophole open to throw me over for somebody else?"

"No, no!" she said. "I have never thought of anybody else. I couldn't imagine myself going with anybody but you. Only I don't want to be tied yet. I want to feel free a bit longer."

"Is that all?" he said, then began to grow angry owing to a reaction from his fright. "A nice fool you would make me look if you turned me down now. I suppose you don't realize that my friends in the train just wink at each other when they ask me to go anywhere of an evening, knowing I shan't go. Then one chap—funny chap he is—always says, 'How's the C.R. doing?' You mayn't know where the joke comes in, but C.R. stands for a railway as well as Carrie Raby. And after all that, I'm to be played fast and loose with. It's carrying things a bit too far. I don't say I agree with the times when men clubbed girls over the head and brought them home like that, but I will say the pendulum has swung too far. A girl can't have a boy of her own and be as free as if she hadn't. I don't know what you think you want, Carrie."

"I've no wish to be horrid, I'm sure," said Caroline. "I do think it is most awfully kind and generous of you to want to give me a ring. But I feel as if I would rather not have one."

"Well, have it your own way, of course. Only I can't make all this out," said Wilf. "If you didn't fancy me for a husband you might have found out before. You've had plenty of time."

"But I never *did* think of you as a husband, somehow," said Caroline. "We began to walk out together like boys and girls do, and it has gone on. I don't say I shall never feel different. I can't picture myself ever wanting to go with anybody but you. Only there it is." She paused, looking out to sea, and the wash of the waves brought back to some degree those feelings which she had experienced when he talked about the five thousand pounds. "I'm sorry if I've hurt your feelings, Wilf. I'm sure I didn't want to. I only wanted to be straight with you."

"Well, we'll let it pass," said Wilf. "Girls have all sorts of funny feelings we don't have, I expect; and a lot would have taken the ring first and talked afterwards. I like a girl to be straight."

But he did not. He was at the stage when what he most wanted from the female sex was a sugared insincerity which looked like crude candour and independence. And as they walked on again, though they were linked together, she certainly appeared less desirable to him than she had done when she was circling round the hall in Wilson's arms with her bright draperies glowing between the gaslight and the sunset.

When they had said farewell at the gate of the Cottage garden and he stood waiting until he heard Caroline safely open the front door, these discontents grew more active still. Here he was, seeing her home, and making no objection, though some one had actually said in his hearing that she was Miss Wilson's maid-servant. He had not told her this from feelings of delicacy, but he began to think that delicacy was rather wasted on her, and determined to do so at the next opportunity.

Caroline opened the door softly and was creeping up the old stairs which creaked at every step, when Miss Ethel peered out of her bedroom and caught a glimpse of flame colour beneath the open coat.

"Good night, Miss Ethel," said Caroline cheerfully.

For a moment Miss Ethel could not bring words over her lips. That Ellen's niece should return thus at midnight, opening the house door with a latch-key, while she, herself, condoned it, though she disapproved as violently as ever. She felt a sort of tingling shame and resentment like a fighter who has to retreat, as she said in a muffled tone: "Good night, Caroline."

Chapter VI
Morning Calls

Miss Ethel was sawing off the dead branch of a tree that threatened to fall on the path when Mrs. Bradford came out of the house and walked slowly across the garden, saying as she passed: "I don't know what you want to do that for, Ethel. You look quite overheated. Why don't you get a man to do it?"

Miss Ethel—beads of perspiration on her flushed forehead and hands trembling with exertion so that she could scarcely hold the saw—replied with pardonable acerbity: "I didn't get a man because I couldn't. You know that. Talk about unemployment! I only know you can't get a jobbing gardener for half a day, even if you put your pride in your pocket and crawl all round Thorhaven on your hands and knees asking one to come as a favour—besides, what would he charge?"

"Well, leave the branch, then," said Mrs. Bradford. "You do worry yourself so, Ethel."

"Somebody must worry," retorted Miss Ethel. Then the bough split unexpectedly and fell, causing her to graze her hand so that it bled. Immediately afterwards there came a loud crash from the other side of the hedge, and for a moment the two women felt their hearts jump with the old sense of helpless, defiant waiting on fate which they had experienced when bombs fell from enemy aircraft during the war. But the next second they remembered they were safe—though that had ceased to be a thing to thank God for.

"It's only a cartload of bricks being tipped," said Mrs. Bradford rather faintly.

"Only!" said Miss Ethel. "Don't you know that means they are beginning to build? And just on the other side of our hedge! And then you calmly stand there and say 'Only!' I wish I were made like you, Marion."

But she very obviously entertained no such desire, and Mrs. Bradford walked on, saying over her shoulder: "I really came out to remind you about going to Laura Temple's. If you really want to see her, it's high time you went."

Miss Ethel pulled her watch out of her belt, glanced at it and hurried indoors, but came out again almost immediately in a hat, with a bundle of papers in her hand. As she went down the road, she—like every one else—

being unable to take in all the impressions that pressed round her, only absorbed those which fed the dominant idea in her mind, automatically neglecting the rest. So when she turned out of the garden gate and caught a glimpse of the cornfields beyond the Cottage where a lark was singing, she missed the idea of permanence—seed-time and harvest never failing—which might have soothed her mind, and only thought how soon these fields too would be built over and spoilt.

Change—change everywhere; not only thrones falling and ancient estates going to the hammer, but little people like herself and Marion all over the world made to feel it every hour. The very spire pointing upwards against the blue-grey sky reminded her less of the eternal message than of something in the service which was different from what it used to be when she was a girl.

But at last she reached a part of Thorhaven which did unconsciously soothe and console her, for it remained just the same: white cottages clustered under high trees and a little house facing the road where Laura Temple lived with an old governess. The house was plain, built close on to the pavement after the old Yorkshire village fashion; and a flagged passage led through it to the garden behind; so when the doors stood open, as now, a blaze of sunlight and clear colour was framed in the further doorway.

While Miss Ethel stood waiting on the step, Laura entered from the garden with some flowers in her hands. "Oh! Do come in, Miss Wilson," she said. "This is nice of you." And she led the way into a square room hung with white curtains and light chintz covers; not an "artistic" room at all, but one which somehow matched the garden outside, as well as Laura herself.

In a well-cushioned chair by the sunny window sat a short, stout lady with very pretty pink hands and faded blue eyes, who rose up from her knitting to greet the visitor. She was the old governess who lived with Laura, and her real name was Panton, but she had always been "Nanty" in the far-off nursery days, and so she was called still by intimates of the family whose various branches she had trained to read and spell. Now she was—as she herself said—eating the bread of idleness; her two great and absorbing interests in life being Laura and knitting. She had been afflicted doubtless with adenoids in her own childhood, but at that time they were not generally considered removable. At all events, she now confused her M's and B's intermittently, as she always had done, and never troubled herself about it, being an easy-going person.

She did not mind, for instance, telling anyone how Laura called to see her one day when she was living in lodgings in Flodmouth, and there and then invited her to come and keep house. But she could not tell what caused this sudden impulse, because she did not know. As a matter of fact, it was just one of those trifles which do influence human conduct by touching the emotions—and always will, let cynics say what they may. And the ridiculous thing which touched this hidden spring in Laura was a very stale, untouched, highly ornamented cake which Miss Panton cut with fingers that trembled from eagerness—so pleased and excited was she by having a visitor at last. "I rather thought I might have had a good bany callers—my papa was so well down here in the old days. But there does not seeb to be anybody left."

The familiar "seeb"—the sudden picture of poor old Nanty waiting there for those callers, descendants of her papa's substantial circle, who never came—the glow of a generous girl newly engaged who wants to make everybody else happy—all this had influenced Laura to say, without waiting to think: "Come and live with me until I am married. I'd simply love to have you, Nanty. Miss Wilson is always saying I ought to have a chaperone since I ceased wandering about and went to live in my own little house at Thorhaven."

So that was how Miss Panton came to be sitting in that pleasant corner of the sunny room, doing her knitting and listening while Laura talked to Miss Ethel about the nursing fund in which they were both interested. Occasionally Miss Panton would push forward mechanically a conversational counter from the little store she kept always by her. Thus when Miss Ethel spoke of the bricks that had arrived on the other side of the privet hedge, Nanty glanced up for a second to remark in her throaty little voice: "It is hard. That lovely garden of yours, Miss Ethel—— But tibe and tide wait for no ban!" Then she sighed and resumed her absorbing occupation, satisfied that she had taken her due part in the social amenities.

This habit of using ready-made platitudes arose no doubt from laziness of mind, as well as from the natural timidity produced by being a nursery governess in days when such unfortunate young females hovered ever uncertainly between basement and drawing-room. She had got into the way then of making remarks at the luncheon table which she knew must be correct, because they were in all the copy-books.

Now she and Laura lived very happily together, and this pleasant feeling was intensified by the rather exaggerated adoration of the girl's lover which such a situation is apt to produce. The little household circled round his goings and comings, and the young mistress of it lavished on Wilson all the family affection she had at the disposal of a large circle, if she had been blest with one, as well as the pure passion of a woman deeply in love.

At last Miss Ethel finished her business, closed her little notebook and made a brisk remark about the building in the next field, because she was always very careful not to hurt Miss Panton's feelings.

"Delightful! Delightful!" said Nanty, seeking the appropriate conversational counter—"at least, I bean——" She paused, breathed hard, and added with a rush: "I'm sure Mr. Wilson was deeply distressed at being obliged to be the one to sell it. But if he had not done so, somebody else would. Business is business," she concluded, pink to the nose-end with the effort.

Laura's colour also rose a little. "Yes. I know Godfrey was sorry. Only he is tremendously keen to get on, of course, and you can't afford—I sometimes think he is too keen."

But Miss Ethel was not going to have that. It must be made plain at once, that though *she*, herself, might run down her own second cousin, he was the sort of man whom any girl ought to be proud to marry, even though she did possess an agreeable sum of money at her own sole disposal. "I have always considered Godfrey a gentleman—if that is what you mean?" she said stiffly.

But Laura was looking out of the window and did not listen. "Oh, here is Godfrey!" she said, jumping up. "Will you excuse me a moment, Miss Ethel?" And she hurried off to prevent an awkward meeting.

But before she reached the door, Godfrey was already in the room— alert, buoyant, with his air of being well fed, well bathed, well groomed and entirely certain of himself. Immediately after greeting Laura, he turned to Miss Ethel. "I am very glad to have come across you," he said, "I am afraid you felt hurt about that field before your house; but the Warringborns meant to sell, so of course I couldn't tell them to take their business elsewhere. And they were urgent, so the whole thing was arranged hurriedly."

Miss Ethel drew down her mouth but said nothing; and before Laura could make some trivial remark Miss Panton nervously filled in the pause by murmuring: "Quite so. Delays are dadegerous."

Then Miss Ethel rose to go, and having recovered herself a little she did manage to say a civil word to Wilson about the weather—because after all he was her kinsman, and must be supported here as such.

A few minutes later, Wilson and Laura followed along the same road. "Then I suppose we may take it that diplomatic relations have now been resumed?" he said with a grin.

Laura smiled—but kindly—feeling some pity for Miss Ethel. "After all, it is hard to have people looking over your hedge when you have always had the place absolutely private. Only she will make such a tragedy of the inevitable."

But Godfrey was not greatly concerned with Miss Ethel's feelings. "I say, Laura," he began eagerly, pointing to some new houses. "There are tremendous opportunities in Thorhaven for a man with capital. If only I had twenty thousand pounds at my disposal, I could be a rich man in ten years' time."

She looked up at him quickly, flushing a little. "Well, you can have, Godfrey. I'd like you to have it. I get possession of my money on my marriage, you know: and, thank goodness, it is not in trust. My father had a perfect horror of leaving things in trust."

"I'm not sure I agree with him there," said Godfrey. "You might have got hold of a chap who would make ducks and drakes of your money. But as things are, it is all right, of course. The only question is—shall you always be absolutely comfortable about it? Because, if you would even feel the very faintest——"

"But I don't! I never shall," interposed Laura. "You know I'd trust you with a million if I had it."

He slipped his hand through her arm, for just then they turned the corner and met the sea wind full in their faces. "Dear old girl: there are not many like you."

Laura felt herself propelled along so easily with his thick-set figure between her and the wind from the sea; the warm vitality that came out from him and seemed to run also through her veins, making her feel stronger, gayer, more exuberantly full of energy than she ever did when alone. She wanted to tell him her feelings, after the way of lovers, and so she turned to him with a little quick pressure of his arm in hers as they neared the pay-box. "Godfrey! I feel as if I could jump over the moon. Don't you? It must be this lovely morning."

He let his glance rove idly over the promenade gardens and the road leading to it, which certainly looked their best on this day of real summer, when there was hot sunshine to warm the breeze, and girls and children in pink and blue and white and yellow playing on the sands. The sea was a sparkling green and a couple of boys ran out into the surf, shouting as they ran.... But though Wilson had an eye for beauty, he was thinking chiefly of the row of villas which could be built where a cornfield now grew—and lodging-houses on the cliff top with steps down from the gardens to the shore—and the money rolling in. Then he heard Laura speaking to the girl in the pay-box as she went through the barrier; and with a sudden jolt of the memory the nymph in the flame-coloured gown came back to mind, though he had forgotten all about her from the night of the promenade dance until the present moment.

He hesitated a few seconds, then he also stepped forward and peered in at the little window with Laura, who was still talking; and instantly, his sudden curiosity fell flat like a bubble pricked. For he saw just enough resemblance in this ordinary, pale, alert little girl, with the bright eyes and the freckles on her nose, to make sure she was the same person, and after that one glance he stood looking away to sea with his hands in his pockets, whistling softly, awaiting his lady's pleasure. He was no longer curious.

Caroline, defiantly aware of all this, answered Laura's pleasant remarks at random. She was not going to have him tell about the red dress in his own way—since he had evidently never thought again of it or her—making a funny tale to amuse Miss Laura—she'd tell it in *her* way! "Miss Temple, I wanted to tell you, I wore that flame-coloured dress you gave Aunt Creddle at the promenade dance the other night. She burnt mine ironing it out, so I borrowed that at the last minute. But I did it no harm and gave it back to her next day." The words came out breathlessly, in a little rush, and the bright eyes peered defiantly through the little window.

"Oh, what a pity to give it back," said Laura. "I expect it suited you, and really I only gave it to Mrs. Creddle, because Mr. Wilson disliked it so much." She smiled round at him, then turned again to Caroline. "Do wear it again, and then I can let you have the shoes and stockings to match. They are such a peculiar shade that they will go with nothing else I have."

"No, thank you," said Caroline abruptly: but the next minute she smiled into the face so near her own, softening her refusal—for she could not help feeling the charm of that open-eyed kindness with which Laura had looked out at the world since she was in the cradle. It was so real: and yet it formed a weak spot in Laura's nature. For she wanted so much to be liked that she was—as some one had once said of her—just a little bit disappointed if a stray cat did not purr as she went past. Now she answered quite eagerly, but with a perfectly genuine eagerness: "Oh, I do hope you'll change your mind. Anyway, I'll send the shoes and stockings, though I'm afraid the shoes will be too big for you."

Then she went off, leaving Caroline tingling from head to foot with annoyance against Wilson. To think he should treat her in that way, as if the dance the other night were something to be ashamed of. Only wait until he tried to speak to her when Miss Temple was not there, and he should see what would happen.

But Wilson was walking by Laura's side on the promenade without the remotest intention of talking to Caroline again: and he had so lost interest in her that he was almost surprised to hear his lady ask how the dress looked.

"I spoke to the girl because I mistook her for you from the back," he said.

"But did she look nice in it?" persisted Laura.

"Nice?" He paused, and she was so tall that his face was almost on a level with her own. Then he glanced back at the pay-box. "Poor little devil! She can't have known herself, if she happened to see her reflection that night. The dress worked miracles. I can hardly believe it was the same girl."

"She is engaged to some young man in an office in Flodmouth, I believe," said Laura. "I wonder if you could do anything for him?"

"I'm afraid not. We don't interfere in each other's office arrangements in Flodmouth business circles," he said, teasing her, though he saw and appreciated that kindness always welling up in her like a spring, ready for every one. "All right, old girl. If I have a chance, I'll do what I can," he added, "but the youth only looks about nineteen, so they have plenty of time yet."

"Nobody has too much time to be happy in," said Laura, smiling at her lover. "Fancy, if we had fallen in love with each other and married ten years ago, we should have been all that to the good."

He laughed. "We might have been all that to the bad," he said. "You don't know what I was like at nineteen, Laura."

So they went along, very happy, laughing and talking together, viewed with envy, contempt or sympathy by the girls and women who read and worked round the band-stand. A thin stream of music drifted out with a sort of melancholy sprightliness to join the deep sound of waves breaking and drawing back from the gravel on the sands. In the distance Caroline looked out from her little window at Wilson's broad back and hated them both, in spite of Laura's kindness. They'd everything—everything. What right had one girl to have so much more than another?... Then a bevy of children came through the barrier, and when she next looked the lovers had vanished.

But later in the morning when Wilson returned home alone by way of the promenade, he glanced at Caroline in passing the barrier with the faintest renewed stirring of curiosity. Surely there must have been something—he couldn't quite have imagined it *all* that night at the dance. Then he saw a bill near the gate announcing another dance this week, and that made him say lightly, as he went through the iron turnstile: "Shall you be at the dance on Thursday? You ought to wear that red dress again."

"No, I aren't—I'm not going to wear the dress any more." She spoke rudely, abruptly—saying to herself that this was what she had expected.

He read her thoughts with ease, smiling to himself, for he knew something about women. But as he looked at her closely in the strong light, he became aware of a velvety texture in her skin which is usually seen only in children. She had a powdering of freckles on her nose, and her pupils had dilated with anger until her eyes looked black; her head was very erect on her slim shoulders. He thought to himself that here were traces of the nymph after all—at least, here was a girl who might conceivably look like one by artificial light and in the right gown. And beyond that, he was vaguely conscious of something in her that was pliant yet unbreakable—or almost unbreakable—and which defied him and all the world.

"What will your other cavalier say to that?" he said. "I expect he will want to see you take the shine out of all the other girls once more."

"Excuse me. There is some one waiting to come through," said Caroline with immense aloofness.

But inwardly she was furious with herself for feeling a just perceptible response to his virile personality and his absolute sureness. Anything he *wanted*—— Then she bent her mind resolutely upon a respected inhabitant of Thorhaven.

"Yes, lovely day, isn't it?" she said. "I suppose you're full up with visitors?"

The woman replied that she was full up, and furthermore that she would remain in the same happy condition until October, then said casually as she moved off: "I didn't know you were living servant with Miss Wilson. I suppose you'll stop there altogether when this job on the promenade is done?"

"I aren't—I'm not living servant with her," said Caroline sharply. "Who's been telling you that? I simply went to light the fire for them in the morning and do a few odd jobs until they could get somebody permanent."

"But I always understood from Mrs. Creddle you were going to be servant there," persisted the woman. "She once told me your aunt Ellen promised years ago."

"Very likely she did," said Caroline. "I can't help that. Everybody must do the best they can for themselves."

"Well, you're right there," answered the woman, and saying Amen thus to the creed of her day, she took up her basket and went through the turnstile.

Chapter VII
Sea-Roke

One afternoon at the turn of the tide, a sort of transformation scene took place along the sands and on the promenade; a bank of cold vapour advanced from the sea, through which the sun glimmered faintly yellow, then disappeared. The girls' thin blouses began to flap limply against their chilled arms; matrons turned a little red or blue about the nose; children's hair either curled more tightly or hung limp, while their cheeks took on a lovely colour in the cool dampness; tiny beads of moisture hung on everybody's eyelashes. Those who had come out to the seaside from the hot streets of Flodmouth felt when they emerged from the railway station, as if they were plunging into a cold vapour bath.

When Caroline went to relieve her colleague Lillie at tea-time, she was met by a stream of nurses, protesting infants and middle-aged women on their way home. And as the men who had just arrived from a day's business in the city made straight for their lodgings, Thorhaven in the very midst of the season took on an air of exclusion—of remoteness. You could notice the wash of the waves again now.

The mist crept steadily along inland, muffling the church, the trees beyond—almost hiding the privet hedge from Miss Ethel as she glanced out of the window.

"A heavy roke. I hope it won't last," she said; but she was not really thinking of what she was saying because her attention was engrossed by the noises on the other side of the hedge. Never the same continuously, but always changing, so that the ear never became dulled by knowing what to expect. A sharply whistled tune. Voices. The knock, knock, knock of a tool on a hard substance. A sound of scraping. Then blessed silence for a few seconds. Then knock, knock, knock again. She turned impatiently to Mrs. Bradford, who sat close up to the window reading the paper. "Thank goodness, it is nearly five; the men will be gone directly."

"You should try to get used to it," said Mrs. Bradford. "You have let it get on your nerves." And she returned at once to the newspaper in which she was reading a minutely-reported divorce case; for though a stolid and intensely respectable woman she loved to read these reports. "It is plain to see that the husband wants to get rid of his wife," she said after a while.

"Well, that seems easily done nowadays," said Miss Ethel, listening still as she spoke. "Perhaps women don't realize that though they can easily get rid of an unsatisfactory husband, it will be just as easy for a satisfactory husband to get rid of them."

But Mrs. Bradford did not care for abstract questions. "I expect the Marchioness will have the custody of the children," she said.

So Miss Ethel took up the other half of the paper to try and distract her mind from the noises over the hedge. But every head-line seemed to dart at her sore consciousness as if it were a snake's head with a sting in it. Murder. Unrest. Strikes. Dissatisfactions. Change. The whole outlook was indescribably comfortless and depressing to her. She felt something akin to the vague, apprehensive misery—beyond reason or common sense—which people feel during the rumble of a distant earthquake.

"I hate reading the papers," she said, flinging the sheet down.

"You shouldn't read the parts that worry you. I don't," said Mrs. Bradford. "But you always were one to work yourself up about things. I remember once how you fretted over some little newsboys with no stockings on, when we went into Flodmouth as children to see the pantomime. You worried yourself and everybody else to death. But they were used to it, as dear father said, and it did them no harm. You are of the worrying sort, Ethel, and you should try to hold yourself in."

"Poor world if nobody worried," said Miss Ethel; then she rose abruptly and carried out the tea-tray.

Soon she was back again with a duster in her hand, beginning to dust the large bookshelf, which had been overlooked for a day or two. As her duster passed over the red-leather backs of the old bound volumes of *Punch* she saw with a wistful inner eye—as if she looked back to a Promised Land on which the gate was shut for ever—that world of swells and belles, of croquet and sunshine, of benevolence to the "poor" and fingers touching forelocks, black being black and white white.

Then Mrs. Bradford spoke again. "Why not leave that dusting, Ethel? You have been at it all day."

"Somebody must," said Miss Ethel, going on dusting.

"Well, I only wish I could do more," said Mrs. Bradford, comfortably turning her page with a rustling crackle. "But my legs have given way ever since I was married. I don't know why, I'm sure; but marriage does seem to affect the constitution in queer ways."

Miss Ethel felt—as she was intended to feel—that it was not within her power to comprehend the mysteries of the conjugal state; so acquiescing from long habit in her sister's torpidity, she went on with her dusting.

But her head ached appallingly, and she looked at the clock-hands nearing five with a feeling that she could bear the sounds of building so long and no longer. If they lasted a single minute beyond that time something inside her head would snap. Knock—knock—knock; scrape—scrape; the thud of something thrown down. She felt her breath coming fast as she waited for the moment when her aching senses would be lulled by the cessation of it all—when she would rest on a blissful silence.

"Thank God, it's five o'clock!" she said, flinging down her duster.

"Yes. The men will be leaving work now," said Mrs. Bradford.

Miss Ethel continued her work again, moving quietly about the room. Wave after wave of wet salt air was rolling in from the sea, pressing upon that which travelled slowly inland, so that the roke grew very dense, and the little house seemed to be cut off from all the world.

Miss Ethel sat down and leaned her head back with her eyes shut: Mrs. Bradford continued to read the paper, then rustled a page and looked at her sister over it. As she did so, Miss Ethel sat up with a jerk and stared across the room.

"Bless me!" said Mrs. Bradford, "what are you staring at me like that for, Ethel? Do I look ill?" And she began to wonder if she felt ill, for she always feared a stroke.

"Listen!" said Miss Ethel in an odd tone. "Don't you hear them? They are working overtime."

Mrs. Bradford took her paper up irritably. "Goodness! Is that all." She also listened, then added: "What nonsense you talk, Ethel! There is not a sound. They have stopped work for the night."

Miss Ethel walked to the window where the grey air clung to the glass and stood there a moment, listening intently. It was true. She could hear nothing.

But as soon as she sat down by the fire and was not thinking, it began again—knock, knock, knock....

"They are there still," she said. "They must be."

"I tell you they are not," said Mrs. Bradford. "You have simply got the noise on your nerves. If you don't take care, you will be really ill. You think about the noise morning, noon and night, until you fancy you hear it."

"I'm not a fool," said Miss Ethel. "Surely I know whether I hear a noise or not."

"I don't know about that," said Mrs. Bradford. "I saw a case in the paper of a man who fancied he heard a drum beating when there was nothing at all, really."

"But I'm not 'a case,'" said Miss Ethel, tartly, pressing her hand to her forehead. "And I'm going to see if the men really *have* left or not."

Mrs. Bradford glanced out of the window. "Well, you must want something to do," she said. "You might just hand me that sheet you were reading, as you go out."

The door banged. Miss Ethel's dim form was visible for a moment as she passed the window then the mist hid her altogether.

Caroline was also engulfed in it as soon as she came out of the little shelter at the entrance of the promenade. She could taste it on her lips, the wet drops clung to her eyelashes. Lillie, who had just arrived to take her place, looked all out of curl like a moulting bird, but both of them were spiritualized by the grey mist which blurred their outlines and through which their lips and eyes showed fresh and wistful.

"Pity you've got your new hat on, Carrie," said Lillie, shaking out her knitted cap. Then she giggled. "But I suppose you were expecting to meet your boy at the train."

Carrie shook her head. "No, I'm going back home first. I have to see about supper."

"I expect you'll take the place on altogether when the season's over," said the girl.

"Not me!" said Caroline, answering the faint echo of condescension in the other's tone. "I've told you time and again, Lillie, how it was I went there. What's more, I'm telling Miss Ethel to-night that I can't stop any longer."

She had not meant to do it precisely on this evening, but suddenly found herself in possession of a full-fledged decision.

"What are you going to do after the prom. closes then," said Lillie.

"Take a post in an office in Flodmouth," said Caroline.

"But you can't do typewriting or shorthand," said Lillie, unimpressed. "You won't find it so easy. I know I had my work set to get a decent job to go to in October, and I'm thoroughly trained. I only took to this on account of my health. I never——"

"You've told me that before," interposed Caroline shortly. "And I can do typewriting. I have been taking lessons with Miss Wannock."

"Well, I wish you luck, I'm sure," said Lillie shortly, shutting down the little window with a click to keep out the damp. She was sufficiently good-hearted, but the trades union spirit was in her and she did not like the idea that another girl should find a post without going through exactly the same training as herself.

Caroline turned towards the main road where nobody could be distinguished twenty yards away and men looked like trees walking; but after a minute or two she noticed something in the general shape and gait of a man coming her way which made her feel sure it was Wilson. She wondered whether he would speak if he caught her up, or whether he would fail to recognize her in the mist, or would give a brief good afternoon and pass on. She slackened speed a little, for though she was still angry with him it would be a "bit of fun" to hear what he had to say. There was also another and far more potent reason. If he walked with her, Lillie would be proved in the wrong; for he would not walk and talk with one whom he regarded as his relatives' maid-servant. But he was nearly past and did not look her way.

"Good evening, Mr. Wilson," she piped then; her voice sounding crudely loud to herself in the grey stillness. But she had to prove her place in the world—make certain of it, lest she should lose it.

"Oh!" He swung round, peering into her face—at first not remembering her. Then something in her bright glance reminded him. "So it is you, is it? Hurrying home to get ready to dance again to-night, I suppose?" He spoke indifferently, disinclined for adventure in the chill, damp atmosphere of this late afternoon. Still he went on, being by nature somewhat expansive. "Is Miss Wilson at home this afternoon, do you know?" then fell into step by Caroline's side without thinking of it.

"Yes. Were you wanting to see her?" said Caroline; but underneath, she was saying to herself: "If I'd done what Aunt Creddle wanted, and been a servant out and out, I should never have walked with Mr. Wilson like this." She felt consciously proud of being a "business girl"—one of the great company that had every evening free, and could wear low necks and powder their faces. But there was more than that in it——

Wilson glanced sideways at her, vaguely satisfied with the lightness of her step by his side and the look of her lips and eyes through the mist. His interest was beginning to wake again. "I am going to the Cottage with some tickets for that Garden Fête for the Hospital which Miss Ethel and Miss Temple are helping to get up."

"Oh, can I take them?" said Caroline.

"No, thank you. I have a message from Miss Temple to deliver as well," he answered.

There was practically no one to be seen on the road—only a few distant objects moving in the mist—and it would have been awkward for either of them to leave the other, so they settled down to walk all the way to the Cottage together.

She spoke abruptly, nervously. "I'm leaving soon, you know. I'm going into an office. I can type, but I can't do shorthand. Still, I aren't afraid of work. If only I could get a bit more practice I should be a very quick typist—the teacher says so."

He walked on, saying nothing, and she thought she had offended him— no doubt he feared she was going to ask him to give her a job. She flushed crimson and added quickly: "I shall find a job all right. A friend of mine is looking round for me."

He turned to her, smiling, and his tone was slightly more familiar than it would have been to a girl of his ordinary acquaintance. "I see. The friend I saw you with at the dance. Well, I hope he'll find what you want."

"I have no doubt he will, thank you," said Caroline.

Wilson was silent for a few minutes. "Look here," he said, "I think we have a spare machine at the office that I could lend you for a time to practise on. You must have practice."

Then he waited complacently for her to swing round towards him—as she did—her eyes and voice filled with surprised gratitude: for he was getting on well in the world himself, and he liked sometimes to feel what a good-hearted fellow he was, in spite of it.

"Oh, that's all right," he said. "But I am sorry you have to leave Miss Wilson."

"So am I, in a way. But you must look after yourself in these days," said Caroline, repeating her formula. "Things aren't like they used to be." She paused. "My goodness, I'm glad they aren't! Fancy if I had had to be another Aunt Ellen all my life."

He laughed, pleased with himself and her. "Well, I must own that I'm glad I was not born into a stagnant world."

A sense of power—of vitality heightened by the stormy times in which they lived, ran through them both as they spoke. It was rather like the feeling of a strong swimmer in a roughish sea, with fitful sunshine and little breakers far out towards the horizon.

By this time they had reached the Cottage and Caroline went in to announce Wilson's arrival. Mrs. Bradford was still reading her paper, but Miss Ethel had not yet returned from her errand to see if the workmen were still working at the new houses.

"I can't think," said Mrs. Bradford, "what Ethel means by going on like this. She just ran out with a shawl round her, and has been absent three-quarters of an hour. I told her the men had stopped work, but she would go to see for herself. I am afraid she may have fallen over a brick or something in the fog." She turned to Caroline. "I wish you would just go and see."

Caroline went out at once and Wilson followed her with a word to Mrs. Bradford. As they crossed the garden the privet hedge loomed like a wall, and above it could be seen the dim outline of brickwork left jaggedly unfinished. Caroline stumbled as she went through the little side gate beyond the hedge, but righted herself immediately, and Wilson withdrew the hand he had put out to help her. Then they walked cautiously among the bricks in the long grass, calling out: "Are you there? Are you there?" But all was dead silence. At last Caroline caught her foot on something soft— dreadful. She had yet no idea why it was dreadful. Then she bent closer. "Miss Ethel! It's Miss Ethel!" She went down on her knees in the long grass. "Miss Ethel! Are you hurt?"

There was no answer, and Caroline said over her shoulder in a quick, low voice: "You'd better go and fetch a doctor. We must not move her until we know if she has broken anything. Send Mrs. Bradford with some rugs."

And though she was so terribly sorry, she was also pleased with her self-control. Aunt Ellen and Aunt Creddle would not have been able to take it like this when they were nineteen. This was what darted through Caroline's mind, even while she spoke.

But the next moment Miss Ethel moaned a little and began to sit up, looking round her affrightedly at the half-built walls in the mist. "What's the matter? What's the matter? I'm on the wrong side of the hedge." Then she remembered and began to shiver violently from head to foot. "I know. I came to see if the men were working. But they were not. The field was all empty. It—I was so sure I heard them—it startled me not to find them here. I think I must have fainted."

"Hush! Don't bother to talk now, Miss Ethel," said Caroline. "You are all right now."

"You are sure you have not broken any bones?" said Wilson.

"Bones? No." Miss Ethel was recovering herself quickly. "It's nothing. I shall be all right in a minute or two. Here, give me your hand, Caroline."

"I daresay you tripped over a brick, Miss Ethel; I very nearly did," said Caroline, helping her to rise.

"Yes, that was it, that was it!" said Miss Ethel, speaking with a sort of exhausted eagerness.

At first as they went up the field she held Wilson's arm, but soon released it and went forward alone. "I'm all right now," she insisted. "Quite all right."

Mrs. Bradford came out into the hall as they entered, and billows of salt mist followed them in. "Shut the door, please," she said. "Then you were not lost, Ethel. What on earth were you doing out there? I began to get quite uneasy about you."

Miss Ethel, turning quickly, gave a look at the two who followed her, but she herself had no idea of its pathos and urgency. "I just tripped on a brick and was stunned for a few minutes—nothing to matter."

So Caroline and Wilson knew they were to let it go at that.

"And had the men gone?" said Mrs. Bradford.

"Yes." She paused. "I thought I would just have a look round."

"You are so restless, Ethel; why can't you keep quiet like me?" said Mrs. Bradford fretfully. "It is a great mercy you didn't break a leg."

Caroline went out of the room to make a cup of tea for Miss Ethel, and when she was lighting the gas-ring Wilson came in hurriedly, saying in a low voice: "I say, you won't mention anything about leaving them to-night, will you!"

"What do you take me for?" whispered Caroline back.

"A girl with her head screwed on the right way," he said. "Then you'll stay and look after them for a little while longer, anyway? I may tell Miss Temple that, may I?"

"You can tell who you like. I shall not mention leaving until Miss Ethel is better," said Caroline.

"Good girl! And I won't forget the typewriting machine," he answered. "One good turn deserves another. That sounds like Miss Panton, doesn't it?" And with that he hurried out of the kitchen.

Chapter VIII
The Height of the Season

The sea-roke lasted for nearly two days and then lifted, the damp, chill air giving place to cloudless sunshine. But even now, when the sun was setting, no cool wind blew in from the sea across the promenade thronged with people in thin dresses. This was so unusual in Thorhaven that those familiar with the place kept saying to each other at intervals: "Fancy being able to sit here at this hour without a coat! The air from the sea puffs into your face as if it came out of an oven———"

The band played outside to-night—not in the hall—and a woman with a good voice strained by open-air concerts during the past summer was singing a song in which the words "love" and "roses" seemed to come with more frequency and on higher notes than the rest, so that they reached the extremist limits of the promenade, floating above the heads of Caroline and Wilf as they sat extended on canvas chairs watching those who walked slowly up and down. It was the night of the visitor *in excelsis*. Stout, important matrons wearing the dresses they had for afternoon calls at home in the towns moved slowly along in small groups, with a solid man or so in attendance who smoked his pipe or cigar and said little, but that little rather jocular. Girls tripped by, either pale with the heat, or flushed, or protected from extremes of temperature by a heavy layer of powder: and flappers with pert faces and fluffy hair swung gaily along, always with a generous display of fat neatly-stockinged leg. But it was all charming, particularly in the evening light, because there was about it all such an appealing atmosphere of youth and summer.

Caroline and Wilf leaned back at their ease in their chairs, making remarks on those who went past. He was tired with the day's work in a stifling office in Flodmouth, and she with her extra household occupations at the Cottage owing to Miss Ethel's indisposition.

"Good thing I happen to be only relieving Lillie this week," she said. "If it had been my turn to stop all day, I don't know what they would have done at the Cottage. But Miss Ethel is better now. I had meant to tell them I was leaving—that night she was taken ill, you know."

"Well, I think it is a pity you hadn't got it done," said Wilf. "They'll be up to any dodge to keep you now. I know 'em." And he shook his head wisely.

"You surely don't imagine Miss Ethel sort of felt I was going to give notice, and so fell down and hurt herself on purpose?" said Caroline, laughing.

But Wilf, pallid and exhausted with a burning day in a Flodmouth office—his nerves slightly upset by too many cigarettes—was in no mood to be chaffed.

"I never gave a hint at anything so ridiculous," he answered fretfully. "I simply say that in my opinion you are not in your right position there, and if you consult my wishes, you'll make other arrangements as soon as possible. I did tell you so before, I think."

"And I meant to do it," said Caroline. "Honour bright, I did." She glanced at him sideways. "I don't care about it any more than you. Only I promised Mr. Wilson I would stop on until Miss Ethel was better."

"Wilson!" said Wilf. "What's he to do with it, I should like to know. He doesn't seem to me to bother much about the old girls as a rule." Then certain vague memories of that dance in the promenade hall which had not been entirely obliterated by Wilson's skilful treatment came back with renewed vividness. "I see what it is; he's after you himself. So long as you stop at the Cottage, he knows where to put his hand on you. You needn't think I was such an owl as not to see he was taken with you that night on the promenade. You know—when you had the red dress on. But you needn't flatter yourself much over that sort of attention, I can tell you. He'd have gone on just the same with any sort of girl out of Flodmouth who happened to take his fancy for the minute. You don't know men of his sort like I do. And now you're silly enough to stop on at the Wilsons just because he asks you: even when I ask you not. It's time you learnt——"

"Don't talk rot!" interrupted Caroline—a sudden heat of anger flushing her all over as she jumped up from her seat. "I'm nothing to Wilson and he's nothing to me. Look there—if you want any proof. That doesn't look as if he had eyes for any other girl but his own, does it?"

Wilf glanced in the direction indicated, and Caroline sat down again. Then they both watched Wilson coming down the promenade with Laura Temple, whose happy face was turned towards her lover with a glow of trust and confidence upon it that no one could mistake: and when he looked at her, his rather coarse-featured, harsh face was softened a little, as if irradiated by that glow. They walked close together, talking gaily as they threaded in and out of the crowd from which advancing twilight had begun to steal the bright colours. Soon all girls wearing white, even those with bold features and exaggerated coiffures, became exquisite in that half light:

and across the still expanse of darkening sea the Flamborough Beacon swung out, white—white—red; a night made for young lovers.

But the two who sat on the long chairs by the rail of the promenade were letting it all go by, engrossed in their own pricking dissatisfaction. "Well, what does it matter to me whether Mr. Wilson and Miss Temple look soppy over each other, or not?" said Caroline. Then she rose again abruptly: "My head aches. I'm tired of watching all these people go past. It makes me feel dizzy. Let's go for a turn on the cliff."

He remained obstinately seated on the canvas chair, his legs stretched out before him. "What's the use? When we've just paid twopence each for our chairs? They'll be snapped up in a minute and we shan't get any when we come back."

"All right. You stop where you are," said Caroline, walking away.

He let her go until she reached the exit that led towards the cliff top, then reluctantly rose from his seat and with long strides caught her up. "Oh, don't you come if you don't want to. I'm all right," she said over her shoulder.

"Don't be soft. People would think we'd quarrelled," said Wilf.

"Let them think, then," said Caroline.

"Oh, that's it, is it?" He stood still. "I can go back if you don't want me, you know. I'm not one to force myself on anybody."

"All right. Go back." They stood on the cliff beyond the promenade peering into each other's angry faces, in the translucent dusk reflected from the great expanse of sky and sea.

"You mean that?"

"Yes, I do."

"You want things to come to an end between us?"

"I'm not particular." She paused, then drew a long breath. "Yes—as you put it like that—I do."

"Well, if you do it now, it's done for good. You won't whistle me back again, you know. I'm not that sort. If I go, I go." He paused, adding with a sudden spurt of anger at her injustice: "And I shan't come back if you crawl on your hands and knees after me from one end of the promenade to the other. I haven't done nothing. What's the matter with you? But I can tell you. You're gone on that Wilson."

"I aren't gone on him," said Caroline angrily. "A man I hardly know. You must have got a bee in your bonnet, Wilf."

"I may, or I may not, but I'm not going to have my future wife conduct herself in a silly style without saying a word," he answered with youthful pomposity.

"Your wife! It hasn't got to that yet," said Caroline. Then she thrust her face nearer to his, adding impulsively: "It would be years and years before we could think of marrying. I didn't plan ahead like that when we started keeping company, and I don't feel as if I could ever look on you as a future husband, Wilf. I don't feel I ever shall want to marry you—not now it comes to it."

"Then that's why you wouldn't have my ring," he said, his face blank and pale in the twilight. He began to see that it was all real—not just a "tiff" such as they had had before.

"I suppose so," said Caroline, her tone changing too—becoming anxious and slightly troubled. "I didn't realize at the time, but I expect I was shying away from the idea, if you know what I mean?"

"Oh, I know what you mean well enough. You're tired of me, and you want to turn me down. But let me tell you you won't find fellows like me growing on every gooseberry bush. I've always treated you like a gentleman—I have. I never hinted a word when you were going out as day girl to that woman who keeps a little shop in your street, though I could see some of my pals thought I was walking out a bit beneath myself. And this is the return I get." He jerked his hat back on his head. "It's enough to make a chap go to the dogs and enjoy himself: blest if it isn't!"

"I'm sorry, Wilf. I know I'm behaving like a perfect pig, but when it comes to marrying, you must have the right sort of feeling, or where are you?" said Caroline.

"Well, I only know one thing. I wish to goodness I had bought that second-hand motor-bike I wanted, instead of saving up the money against getting married! Why, I fair couldn't sleep for thinking about it: and now Simpson has bought it. And it was all for you. And now this is how I'm treated."

"Oh, Wilf! You never told me. I never knew about the motor-bike," said Caroline, taken aback.

"There's lots of things you don't know about," said Wilf. "However, if you're bent on ending it all, I shan't try to stop you. *I* aren't one to force myself upon a girl that doesn't want me."

Caroline's lip began to tremble "Wilf, if I'd known about you giving up the motor-bike I wouldn't never have spoken as I did. I do feel a beast. But you have to think about yourself in this world or nobody'll think for you. I can't see any reason in going on as we are doing for years and then getting married when we're both dead sick of it all and of each other. We only keep each other back. We should be better free."

"Meaning you want to be free?" He had to pause a minute, owing to a thickness in his throat. "All right. I shan't hold you to it. You go and see if you can find a chap that can marry you straight off. That's what you want. You'd never have broken with me if I'd had a big house and plenty of money. I should not have been too young for you then. You'd not have had to chuck me over then, to better yourself."

She was weeping now—very grieved to hurt him, and yet, beneath her softness, an iron determination to do what was best for herself; no thought of sacrifice because of his pain entering her head. "I'm so sorry, Wilf. I'm so sorry," she murmured.

But he felt she was implacable. She was armoured by that phrase of hers, she'd "got to do the best for herself," and he knew he had no weapon to pierce that armour.

They both stood on the edge of the cliff in silence, looking towards the north where the Flamborough lights gleamed out at regular intervals across the dark water. The promenade lay behind them, a fringe of pale lights twinkling along the shore.

Caroline was crying for the sorrow she had given Wilf, but that only lay on the surface, though genuine enough. Beneath that, all unknowing, she mourned a loss which nothing could restore. She and Wilf had given each other that first bloom of young attraction—bright glances, touches, cool kisses almost without passion—and no power could bring that back. They felt miserable, standing there with the little waves coming in—whish! whish!—upon the gravelly patch of sand: for there lay at the bottom of their hearts a sense of something irretrievably wasted, which they could never have in life any more.

"Well." He spoke first, bitterly. "I hope you may get your rich chap. As you've no more need for me, I may as well go."

"I'm not throwing you over for that, Wilf," said Caroline in a low voice.

His subdued mood spurted up with a sudden irritability of jarred nerves again. "Then what are you for? That's what I should like to know."

"I—I——" She sought to give him a true answer. "You're not old enough. I want a man, now I'm older. You won't be twenty-one for two years."

"A man!" He swung round towards her, peering with fury through the twilight into her face. "A man! What d'you call me? What do you take me for? A man!" He paused, choking for breath, then shouted out: "Go and find your man, then. I don't want you, I don't want you. I wouldn't have you at a gift. A man! Not if you went down on your hands and knees——" He was walking away as he spoke, shouting over his shoulder, almost incoherent with the rage engendered by that sudden stab in his tenderest spot. Just before he was beyond ear-shot, he paused a second and called out: "There'll be no going back. You needn't think it. I shall pay the first instalment of a new bike in the morning."

So the dusk swallowed up his slim figure, and she was left by herself on the cliff. After a while a couple came along closely entwined and when they were close on her the girl said with a start: "Carrie? Is that you all by yourself? Where's Wilf?"

"Oh, he is a bit further on," said Caroline, striving to make her voice sound casual. "Don't you stop for me."

"All right! So long as you haven't pushed him over the cliff, Carrie," said the girl, laughing: then she and her young man went their way, forgetting all about other people.

Caroline waited until they had gone some little distance before she followed them, and as she walked alone on the cliff path with the stars coming out, she had the strangest feeling of loneliness—of lacking something that had always been there since she grew up. It was rather as if she had cast some article of clothing which she had been in the habit of wearing.

On reaching the more crowded part of the cliff near the promenade her first instinct was to keep out of sight; for she had no young man with her, and vaguely felt that she would look odd without one at this time of night. It seemed so "queer" to be walking by herself on the cliff in such an evening hour—but a further strangeness came with the thought that she actually did not possess a "boy" at all. Nobody to wait for her at the gate when she went out in the evening. No one to hang round the pay-box at the promenade entrance to take her home. The sense of missing something was a great deal stronger now than the sense of freedom; she almost wished she had kept in with Wilf, despite that other feeling that made her desire to break with him.

It was a relief to mingle with the crowd coming out from the promenade, because people might suppose she had just left her post at the gate; but she still kept that odd sensation—lightened of a weight, and yet comfortless—as if she had "cast" something which had been more necessary to her than she ever realized.

Chapter IX
Wedding Clothes

Miss Ethel was walking up and down the garden with Laura Temple, both talking.

"I heard Caroline practising on the typewriter as I came through the hall. The kitchen door was open," said Laura.

"Yes. She goes out much less now than she used to do. I fancy she has broken off her engagement with that young man."

"I'm glad Godfrey thought of lending her a machine, for it may make her more satisfied to remain with you; but I daresay that was his idea," said Laura. "He is like that."

"Is he?" said Miss Ethel rather shortly, and added after a moment: "It was very kind of him, of course." She paused again, then broke out vehemently: "I hate and detest all this conciliating and kowtowing. If only I could manage the work myself, I wouldn't do it."

"But you can't—at least, not in this house," said Laura. She also paused, looking deprecatingly at Miss Ethel. "Now, in one of those little new houses in Emerald Avenue, you might manage all right."

"Oh, well, there are none to let," said Miss Ethel, "so that is out of the question."

"But there is one for sale," said Laura: and with that she put her hand through her companion's arm. "Miss Ethel," she went on rather timidly, "Godfrey was wondering if anything would induce you to sell the Cottage. He says he can get a most splendid price for it just now, if you cared to sell. A man who made a tremendous lot out of trawlers or something of that sort in the war is ready to give almost anything you like to ask for it. And Godfrey could offer you a house in Emerald Avenue with vacant possession. You would be quite comfortable there, besides having so much less work."

"Why didn't Godfrey come and tell me that himself, instead of sending you to do his job?" said Miss Ethel. "But his commercial instinct is his ruling passion, of course. He'd make use of anything or anybody for business purposes." She waited a second, then burst forth: "He'd tan his grandmother if he could get a connection by selling her skin."

"You do him a great injustice," said Laura indignantly. "If he did not consider this a good thing for you, he would never have suggested it."

"Well, perhaps not," responded Miss Ethel, exercising great self-control; for she remembered that Godfrey was a Wilson, while the girl to whom she spoke was after all not one yet. "I dare say he means it for the best. But I'd rather starve here than live in Emerald Avenue. Please tell him that. I'm not so fond of my fellows that I could tolerate hearing the next-door neighbour snore through the bedroom wall—which I understand you can do in these houses, if he snores loud enough. I'm used to a decent privacy." She paused. "I couldn't stand it, Laura," she added in a different tone. "Let us talk about something else. I want you to come indoors and see your wedding present."

Laura turned her brown eyes full upon Miss Ethel, flushing a little and smiling happily. She wore a rough tweed which exactly suited the slight angularity and awkwardness of her tall figure, making it seem just the kind of figure which every English girl living in the country ought to possess, and her voice, always lovely, took on an added sweetness as she said quickly: "Doesn't it seem strange that a month to-day I shall be married? I can hardly believe it."

Miss Ethel responded to that rather bleakly, but asked Laura to come and inspect some china on the kitchen dresser from which she might choose her wedding present.

As they entered the kitchen Caroline answered Laura's greeting civilly, but she did not rise; and while the two stood looking at the pretty Dresden china cups, with their backs turned towards her, she continued her typing. Then after a while Miss Ethel went away to fetch some small silver teaspoons bearing the Wilson crest which she intended to give with the cups, so Caroline and Laura were left alone for a few minutes.

"I see you are practising hard," said Laura. "I hope the machine goes well." She glanced at the pretty cups. "I do seem to be lucky, don't I?"

"Yes. You're one of the lucky ones," said Caroline. But though she smiled, there was a sound of bitterness in her tone which Laura was quick to feel and understand. Poor child, it must seem a bit hard to see another girl having a lover like Godfrey, and lovely presents, and new clothes. Then a sudden kind thought came into her head. "Miss Raby, I wonder if you would care to have a look at my trousseau? I am showing it to my friends next week. Could you come in for half an hour?"

Caroline hesitated, but the "Miss Raby," and the utter absence of patronage, or of any other feeling but sheer good-nature, dispersed her prickly fear of being condescended to, though she only answered rather nonchalantly: "Thank you, Miss Temple, I should be pleased to have a look at your things."

"That's right. What day can you come?" said Laura. "Will Tuesday do?"

"I am on duty all day next week, excepting for meal-times, but I could get in for a few minutes about five," said Caroline.

Very soon after that Laura went away, and a little later, Miss Ethel herself came out of the door, walking slowly across the garden because she did not yet feel at all well. As she went, she noticed for the first time a little flag flying on the roof-beams of the new house that was being built just over the privet hedge. It flapped gaily in the sea-breeze, and seemed to Miss Ethel's irritated perceptions an impudent flag, though she did not formulate her thoughts and was conscious only of a sense of annoyance when she caught sight of the bright patch of colour.

As she glanced up the long hot road outside the garden, her heart almost failed her: but she had collected for the Flodmouth hospital for the past twenty-five years, and a strong sense of duty urged her to continue—especially now that the people from whom she generally collected were less able to give, and more houses had to be visited. But she was not uplifted by any feeling of self-righteousness, because it was just one of the things you did—and there was an end of it. It was a part of the system of life on which she had been brought up.

Half-way between the Cottage and Emerald Avenue she saw the Vicar on the other side of the road. His first impulse was to hasten past without speaking, because he had grown rather weary of her constant diatribes against the changed state of the world; for he too had his full share of the discomforts which come from living in an age of transition, so he felt no desire to hear Miss Ethel press the point home. However, she had been ill and he must do the polite. But as he expected, she at once began. In answer to his inquiries about her health, she said abruptly: "Of course, I'm depressed. How can one be anything else with the world as it is? Nobody seems to be happy here, or to be sure of happiness hereafter."

"You won't mend it by being miserable," said the Vicar, rubbing his lean chin. "I know many feel that it is wrong to be happy with so much injustice and misery about, and there is a great danger that the best souls—who feel this most—may therefore give up creating happiness. But that is just the same as if the violets gave up smelling sweet because of the stenches that abound everywhere. Joy after a while will leave us if we are not careful—then we shall have nothing left but bitterness and pleasure."

"Pleasure is all people want nowadays," said Miss Ethel.

"But you are one of the people—and what do you want?" said the Vicar. "No, Miss Ethel; there are now more men and women in the world wanting to make things right for everybody than ever before in the history of mankind. I sometimes feel as though I could see all the millions just waiting to be shown how to do it. One wonders——" He broke off, flushing a little, and added rather awkwardly: "Well, I must be getting on. I'm glad to hear you are better."

Miss Ethel continued her walk, pondering the Vicar's words. Was the man thinking about the second coming of Christ?... And she remembered how a nursemaid had read some magazine aloud to her long, long ago by the nursery fire in which the very day and hour of the end of the world were given. How she had trembled afterwards at the tipping of a load of bricks in the road forbear that was the Day of Judgment beginning. Then her thoughts came back again to the present. Was it true that all these millions were waiting for a leader? Faith seemed to be dying everywhere. Everything was different—everything was different.

The words drifted achingly through her mind as she turned into the gate of a largish house facing the main road, opening her collecting-book as she went, so as to be ready with the name and amount. At once she began to adjust her mind, ready for the short chat with the lady of the house which was a necessary accompaniment of her round.

But it would be easier than usual to-day, for a topic was ready to hand— most of the ladies on whom she called taking a lively interest in the Temple-Wilson wedding, anxious to know if Miss Ethel had seen the bride lately, and if it were true that the trousseau surpassed all previous ones ever seen in Thorhaven.

This interest was so widespread, indeed, that on Tuesday afternoon when Caroline remarked just before leaving the pay-box on the promenade that she was going to have a look at Miss Temple's wedding outfit, the girl who took her place immediately went through varying stages of surprise, curiosity and envy. "She asked you! Well, you've got something out of living with those old women for once. I wish I was going too!"

"Wish you were!" called back Caroline, insincerely. But as she went alone down the road to the little house at the other end of the village, her own desire to see the trousseau died away, so that when she stood on the threshold looking through at the patch of bright garden through the farther door, she began to wish she had not come. As she stood there, Laura came from the garden, in which the colours were less delicate, more vivid than before, but they still bloomed with the peculiar, clear brightness which flowers seem to gain which have survived the sharp spring of the East Coast.

"Oh! I am so glad you could get off, Miss Raby," she said. "Shall we go straight up and see the things before tea?"

"I was going home to tea," murmured Caroline, a little abashed, yet angry with herself for feeling so.

"You would not have time," said Laura, leading the way. "Please stay. I was expecting you for tea."

Then they were in the room: and Caroline drew a long breath when she saw the lovely garments spread forth on the bed and on the chairs and tables. They were so exquisite in stitchery and in the fineness of the material, that no girl who loved pretty things could look at them without enjoyment; therefore Caroline's "Oh, Miss Temple, I never, never saw anything so lovely!" was entirely natural and spontaneous.

Laura stood smiling and a little flushed in the midst of her dainty garments; and the room seemed at that moment to be full of a very charming atmosphere of girlish admiration and pleasure. One after another the filmy things were touched softly or held up to the light, while the two pairs of eyes—one pair deeply glowing and the other wide and bright—met over them in sympathetic appreciation.

"But this is the sweetest of all," said Laura happily. She was delighted to be giving pleasure, but—beneath that—she equally enjoyed indulging her desire to be liked by everybody. As she spoke she lifted from the bed where it lay a most exquisitely embroidered dressing-gown with a little cap to match.

"Yes, lovely," said Caroline. But the alteration in her tone was so marked and so sudden that Laura turned round quite sharply to see what the matter was: and in so doing she caught something clouded—sullen—what was it? just passing across the other girl's face. Why, of course—how dreadfully hard to see somebody else having all these beautiful things while you had nothing! Her sudden realization of this point of view was so complete that she flushed deeply from chin to forehead. What a perfect idiot she had been—when she only meant to be kind.

All the same she was now mistaken; that change in Caroline's expression being caused by something entirely different from what she imagined herself to have discovered; and she would have been both startled and surprised had she known the actual fact. As it was, her one desire was to somehow retrieve her mistake. She looked at her pretty things, trying eagerly to think of something that she could give without seeming to patronize, and her glance fell on a box of coloured handkerchiefs, so she took it up in her hand and said carelessly: "Oh! these don't belong here. A firm from whom I bought a great many things sent me them, and they are a kind I never use. Still I had to keep them. I wonder if you would take them with you out of the way?"

"Very kind—I'm sure. But you'll find a use for them," murmured Caroline, not extending her hand. The two girls looked away from each other, both a little discomfited; and in doing so they saw a photograph of Wilson in a silver frame which had been covered up and which the removal of the handkerchiefs had left exposed.

In that brief silence the atmosphere subtly changed, though neither exactly realized that it had done so.

"Well, I'm afraid I must be going now, Miss Temple," said Caroline. "Thank you very much indeed for letting me see your things." And she moved towards the door.

"You are forgetting your handkerchiefs," said Laura, pressing them into Caroline's hand. "Do have them, just to please me. But you must have a cup of tea before you go. It is all ready."

With that she led the way into the sitting-room, and Caroline lacked the social address to disentangle herself from the situation without being actually rude. She did not want to be that, therefore followed Laura, and as they went into the room Wilson rose from a seat by the window. But his heavy figure was silhouetted with a sort of hazy, golden outline against the strong afternoon light, and so she could not see his expression.

"Been viewing the marvels upstairs, Miss Raby?" he said easily, as she shook hands with Miss Panton. "Take this comfortable chair, won't you? It must be an exhausting job."

"No, have this; you'll find it much nicer," said Laura, laughing. But as they stood together, making much of Caroline, she saw that the chair Wilson had indicated was evidently one sacred to himself. The long, low seat, and the small table near containing cigarettes, ash-trays, pipes, and other conveniences, all pointed to the same care on the part of these two women.

Caroline sat down on the chair offered by Laura and crossed her feet with aggressive nonchalance because she was feeling nervous. "Anyway, this is a good deal different to mine on the prom.," she said, suddenly anxious to let Miss Panton clearly understand that she was the girl on the promenade, and not Miss Wilson's servant.

Miss Panton looked at her over the teacups and said: "Sugar? Bilk?" with the catarrh very much in evidence.

"I didn't tell you, Miss Raby, did I, that Miss Panton has given me a foot-muff for the car?" said Laura, speaking rather quickly, conscious of some odd constraint in the air. "We are going for a motor tour in the Lake District for our honeymoon. Every one says it is ideal in September. I have never been, oddly enough."

"Well, the glut of honeymooning couples in the Lakes is now a thing of the past," said Wilson, smiling at his future bride. "There was a time when a certain hotel at Windermere swarmed with them, I believe. Everybody looking out of their eye-corners at breakfast time to see if she knew how many lumps of sugar he took in his coffee."

Miss Panton murmured something about Wordsworth, obviously thinking that a more fitting topic to be discussed before a young person who was taking tea on sufferance with her betters.

"Perhaps Miss Raby is like me, and doesn't care much for Wordsworth," said Laura, looking across at her guest in a very friendly fashion. "I never got beyond 'We are seven,' and never wanted to."

"It's never too late to bend," retorted Miss Panton, still austere; her glance resting with deep disapproval upon the neatly stockinged leg which Caroline displayed.

"Come, Nanty," said Laura, laughing. "Don't be so superior. You know you don't really care for anything but a love-story with a happy ending yourself." She paused, looking round at them with her happy, brown eyes: "Well, there isn't anything better: is there?"

"Of course not," said Wilson, just touching Laura's shoulder as he passed her in handing the cake to Caroline. But as he did so his glance met Caroline's by chance, and he became instantly aware that she had been watching him, for she looked hastily away, while a colour which she could not control came into her cheeks, deepening and deepening until it almost brought tears to her eyes.

She sat near the window with the full light on her face, somehow oddly defenceless in her extreme embarrassment, and he could see the light powdering of freckles on her nose, as well as that curious, camellia-petal fineness of skin which always escaped notice until the observer came quite close, for there was a tinge of sallowness in the colour which prevented people from admiring it at first sight.

But a decent man who is to be married in a month does not, of course, indulge in speculations about another girl's complexion—at any rate, he does not encourage himself in doing so—and very soon Caroline removed temptation out of his way by rising and taking her leave.

As she said good-bye, the lovers stood in the doorway with the sunshine on their faces and the bright flowers seen through the far door behind them. She was glad to get away, her mind in a whirl of gratitude, defiance, curiosity and envy which bewildered herself. Of course, it was nice of Miss Temple to ask her to tea and treat her like any other girl friend, but anybody could be nice when they were getting everything in the whole world that they could want.... Her thoughts paused on that. That *didn't* always make people kind——

She started at the sound of the church clock and began to run, lest she should be late for the promenade.

But when she arrived her budget of news proved very disappointing to the expectant Lillie, who had lingered round the pay-box with her own tea waiting at home in the hope of hearing in more detail what every separate garment was like. But when she at length extracted the information that Wilson was also there, and that the party had taken afternoon tea together, her curiosity became intense.

"Did they look as if they were awfully gone on each other? I always thinks she seems sweet, and I think he ought to consider himself lucky, don't you? I say, fancy if you or I were in her place and going to be married next month? Feel funny, wouldn't it? But I shouldn't care much to be taking him on, should you? Too jolly cocksure for me."

"Chance is a bonny thing," said Caroline shortly. "I'll shut the door if you don't mind. There's a fearful draught blows through this place with it open."

The girl went round to the turnstile on her way out and addressed a last remark to Caroline through the little window. "You needn't be chippy with me because you haven't got twelve of everything all hand-embroidered. It isn't my fault!" she flung over her shoulder.

And having thus revenged herself for her colleague's uncommunicativeness, she went her way.

Caroline, left alone in her chair before the little window, automatically scanned the faces of those passing through the barrier, ready to release the clutch with a "Good evening" if the person were known to her, or to say in a dull monotone, "Six-pence, please," to a stranger. Every now and then she glanced at the darkening sky towards the North where clouds were gathering up, and after a while, single drops of rain began to fall. Very soon the empty promenade glittered black under a downpour, the lights making streaks of pale gold across it. People only came in now at infrequent intervals; a few dark figures hurried along the promenade; while the sound of the band in the covered hall drifted across through the open windows, mingling with the deep voice of a storm rising far out at sea.

After a while Wilf passed through, ostentatiously indifferent. "Oh, that you, Carrie? Good evening, I didn't see it was you at first. Beastly night, isn't it?" And he went on jauntily, sticking his hands in the pockets of his mackintosh.

Caroline watched him go with a most illogical sense of being deserted; then the turnstile clicked and she had to release the clutch, letting through a pleasant-looking mother with a daughter of about seventeen, both so happy in each other's company—making a lark of coming out together to hear the band on such a wet night. Caroline's unreasonable feeling of being alone and deserted deepened. For the first time in years, she consciously wanted her own mother—longed for her with an ache of the heart that almost brought tears. She seemed so alone. Aunt Creddle was goodness itself, but had her own family to think of first, of course, and could no longer take quite such a vivid interest in a niece as when her own children were quite little. Uncle Creddle had a steady kindness which nothing could change, but he too was a struggling man with a family. Besides, he was rather hard in some ways beneath his good-nature. She still remembered how he had spoken to her that evening when he found her screaming and playing about those empty houses with the boys.

No, she belonged nowhere: that was it. She did not think as the Creddles did about lots of things, and yet she did not belong to the world which girls like Miss Laura Temple lived in, either. She had got past one sort, and had not found another. All these thoughts passed confusedly through a mind that had been quickened by something incomprehensible in her experiences at Laura Temple's that afternoon. Through her thoughts she heard the hum of the sea, the tinkling fall of heavy rain on asphalt, the faint rising and falling of violin music.

She felt a sudden spirit of rebellion. Why shouldn't she have some fun? She would enjoy herself! She wasn't going to go on like this, letting people in to the promenade, doing housework, practising typewriting. Why did some girls get everything, like Laura Temple, and others nothing? It was not fair. It was not fair——

Then she saw Wilson at the little window. "Good evening. Stormy night!" he said, and passed through without any further remark.

She knew he had come straight from Laura's and was taking a short cut across the parade to his own lodgings, which were beyond the exit towards the north. He had come from no desire to see her. Still he might have spoken a word: he need not have gone through like that, as if it were only Lillie working the turnstile.

As she thought that, she felt a tear on her lips. Licking it off, she demanded furiously of herself how she could be such a fool as to cry about nothing. She must be run down. She must want a tonic.

Then she glanced up at the sound of a step approaching from the promenade, and there was Wilson's face, quite near, looking in at her little window. "You'll have a wet walk home, I'm afraid," he said.

"Yes." Her voice held a faint surprise, for he had already spoken once about the weather. "But I have an umbrella here."

"That's a good thing." He hesitated. "I might have lent you one, only it is rather large for a little girl," he added, speaking with a sort of artificial jocosity. "You must find that road rather dark and lonely on a night like this?" He paused again. "Don't you?"

For a moment or two she did not speak, and that silence somehow gave her answer an undue significance. "Yes," she said at last.

He opened his lips to speak, then suddenly his expression changed and he moved away from the window. "Wretched night! Wretched night!" he said, walking briskly on.

Caroline sat back in her chair, almost feeling as if she had been struck in the face—for a question had been asked and answered during that silence which involved all sorts of joys, fears, infidelities; then in a minute he banished them so utterly that she could scarcely believe they had ever been in question.

The next moment Mr. and Mrs. Graham were at the window. "Oh, dreadful night, is it not? You must feel the wind here."

Then they were merged into the shadow of the hall, warning each other as they went along against taking cold. Caroline saw what had happened now. Wilson had no doubt caught sight of the Grahams over his shoulder, and had not wished them to see him talking to her.

Very well!—she was in a flame from head to foot—very well! When he *did* want——

But beneath all that she sensed a weak longing for him which she was trying to drown in a flood of exaggerated indignation. Something told her that when he did want to speak to her again she would not be able to refuse: for he was not only a man for whom she felt a personal attraction, but he was also a type towards which all her new ambitions aspired. Poised as she now was, between what she had left and where she desired to be, he represented to her an ideal—assured, educated, a gentleman.

But though he did not walk home with her—in spite of what he said of the lonely road—she was not to go by herself after all. For a young man who was a connection of the Creddles—a railway porter by trade—chanced to pass just as she was leaving the promenade, and escorted her as far as the gate of the Cottage. He was a good-looking, intelligent youth, with a pleasant, hearty manner and a fair share of those solid qualities which adorned Mr. Creddle—the very man to make a good father and a good husband. Already attracted by Caroline, he would have gone further that night if he had not been discouraged, but she thought of his broken and blackened finger-nails, and of the noise he made when he drank tea, and so they parted at the gate without anything definite being said.

But as she ran up the garden path with her self-esteem thus agreeably restored, she had not the faintest idea that she had just passed by that rarest thing in life—a chance of real happiness.

Chapter X
Sunday Night

The long street leading to the church was thronged with people who walked slowly, smiling and talking to each other, either going towards the lanes beyond the little town, or towards the sea. But a third sort, much smaller in number, threaded rather quickly in and out of the gently-moving crowds with an air of obeying some purpose within themselves and not merely enjoying the lull in the wind at sundown and the warm air. And above it all, clanging out from the grey tower, the last bell rang out a single note urgently: "Come! Come! Come!"

A good many did not notice the bell at all; others just took it in as a sound of Sunday evening which ministered pleasantly to their agreeable feeling of having nothing to do but enjoy themselves; scarcely anyone was troubled by declining that invitation, because the habit of church-going has fallen from the position of a duty to that of a compliment which the religiously disposed are willing to pay their God if quite convenient.

Caroline walked briskly, now and then glancing up at the clock on the tower as if she belonged to the purposeful minority which was making its way to the grey porch. Not that she had started out with any intention of going to the service, but her girl friend had come across an admirer at the church corner, and so it became necessary to do something in self-defence. Impossible to contemplate wandering alone on a Sunday evening without a companion of any sort. The lack of a "boy" for such a purpose made Caroline feel oddly self-conscious—as if people were staring at her and wondering. She would have been glad of the young railway porter's company now, if he had turned up, and would have welcomed him as a sort of refuge.

He sat and smoked on a bench by the sea front, however, all unaware of the opportunity that was rushing past him, never to return. At the last insistent "Come!" Caroline caught sight of Lillie with a young man rounding the next bend of the road, and the idea of being pitied for her solitary condition made her march straight up the flagged path to the church door, as if she had meant going ever since leaving home.

But once inside the church, she experienced a gradual cessation of that prickling awareness of other people's thoughts and other people's eyes which had been so uncomfortable on the road. For she was familiar with the service—having gone to the Sunday school in childhood and attended church at times since, though the Creddles were chapel folk—so that the places in the Prayer Book came automatically to her fingers, and the soothing flow of the words gave her a chance to come to herself. She did not worship in any real sense of the word, but her mind was, despite itself, attuned to peace. "From all the perils and dangers of this night——" Then, after an interval during which the sunset struck golden across a tomb in the chancel: "The grace of our Lord Jesus Christ ... now and for evermore. Amen."

She rose from her knees and her glance fell upon Miss Ethel, who sat a fair distance away in the sparsely filled side aisle. She wondered whether Miss Ethel were a really religious sort or not—you never heard her mention a word about it, and she seemed so up against everything——

Then the hymn—old-fashioned because the Vicar was away and the elderly organist who had chosen it liked that kind best. Perhaps he knew that all religion must at the last be a matter of feeling and not of reason, for he had lived such a long time in the world and really loved God. But the strange preacher who was going to occupy the pulpit looked down the church at the congregation singing and felt they required a great deal of sound teaching. So, being a good man with a high ethical standard, he stepped up into the pulpit and did his best during the opportunity which was at his disposal to correct the effect of what he considered sentimental doggerel.

But as Caroline listened to him, she felt his explanations of a reasonable faith washing away from her mind all the beautiful pictures which had been stored there and had formed part of her life, though she had not valued them. No doubt he meant well; still the explanations took away and gave nothing to fill the empty place. Soon her mind wandered and she caught sight of a hat trimmed in a way that was exceedingly smart and easy enough to copy; so that occupied her attention until she heard the familiar rustle among the congregation and the "Now" which gives release.

The clergyman stood near the east window to give the blessing with a side light slanting across his white surplice, and a thought darted into Caroline's mind, turning her hot from head to foot—Why, that was just how the Vicar would stand with the bride and bridegroom before him at the altar-rails in three weeks' time! And a vision of Laura in her veil beside Wilson's broad, strong figure gave her a queer, unhappy feeling of irritation and pain; yet somehow she wanted to indulge the pain—to press it in upon her senses by dwelling on it.

Then her healthier instincts suddenly revolted. "It's nothing to me. I aren't jealous of another girl getting married! I could be married myself to-morrow if that's all." But deep within her she felt it was not all; so rising abruptly she went out, not looking again at the chancel.

Miss Ethel came forth more deliberately, nodding to one here and there among the townspeople as she passed under the porch into the cool evening, but her salutations were not acknowledged with the appearance of gratification or respect which she had seen accorded to her parents years ago—young people from shops and post-offices nodded off-handedly back, or at most gave a somewhat condescending "Good evening, Miss Wilson," feeling in their confident youth and independence that it was they who had done her the favour.

It was all so different; that constant burden of her thoughts—— And as she walked home through the end of the sunset, the forlorn restlessness of the cat turned out of its basket and forced to wander in cold, strange places seized upon her again. She could not formulate her unease excepting by that one phrase: it was all so different.

When she reached home, Mrs. Bradford looked up with a sort of solid expectancy: "Well, did you have a good sermon?"

"I suppose so. The Vicar was not there. The man we had explained to us that there was no heaven and no God, so I suppose he was very clever."

Mrs. Bradford stared, then relaxed comfortably into her cushions once more. "Oh, you mean he held those new views about religion," she said. "I have just been reading a novel that has something about that in it. Was he young? I always like a young preacher, because their voices are generally stronger and you can hear better."

Miss Ethel had gone to the window and now stood there, looking out. The eyebrow which was affected a little by emotion or excitement gave a slight twitch occasionally and her lips were pressed close together. She saw the little flag on the roof over the privet hedge hanging quiet on the still air, and it added to her sense of being conquered by those forces which had been creeping on steadily, bit by bit, until she could not ignore them any more than the new houses.

But she had never before felt it as she did to-night, looking up at that exquisite clear sky with the sickle moon rising. She was not well, tired with the walk and the service; and a most unwonted pressure of tears ached behind her eyes, though she fiercely fought against them.

"Ethel!" said Mrs. Bradford. "What are you standing there for? Why don't you go and take off your things for supper?"

"I am going." Miss Ethel controlled her voice to speak as usual. "I'll just put the kettle on first, because Caroline won't be in for some time yet." And she began to cross the room, when suddenly, abruptly, she stopped short. Standing quite still in the midst of all those heavy chairs and tables that gleamed dimly in the falling dusk, she blurted out in a queer, strangled tone: "I hated that sermon. I don't think clergymen ought to be allowed to preach like that. They want to change God. They can't even leave God the same."

"You really do upset yourself about things so, Ethel," said Mrs. Bradford fretfully. She wanted her supper. "What does it matter to you what other people think? You should just take no notice and go on in your own way, and believe what you always have believed—as I do."

Miss Ethel made some inarticulate reply, and went out to put on the kettle. Not for any earthly consideration would she have told her sister that that was exactly what she could not do: that because she listened carefully to sermons and read articles about religion the unchanging God was gradually giving place to a vague Power which nebulously adapted itself to the needs of a changing civilization.

The gas-ring spurted under the match in her hand, lighting up with a bluish light her pale, thin face. Her lips moved as she murmured to herself for comfort: "The *same* yesterday, to-day and for ever." But she could not find anything to hold on to in that any more.

Then she heard an unexpected sound at the door, and the next minute Caroline came in, drawing off her gloves.

"I'll see to the hot water, Miss Ethel," she said.

"You are in early to-night," said Miss Ethel.

"Yes." Caroline paused. "Oh, I have been going to tell you that I shall——" But with the words nearly over her lips, she found herself unable to speak them. "Shall be late in to-morrow," she substituted; for somehow she could not after all cut herself adrift from this house yet, though she came fresh from a conversation which had left her burning with annoyance.

She tingled still at the recollection of one girl saying to another in passing: "That's Caroline Raby! What's she doing? Oh, she's in service." And at the memory of her own sharply-flung: "I'm not in service, then! I take tickets on the promenade and I'm going into an office after that."

But though it was evident that she was regarded by some as being in service, and though she felt no higher regard for it than anyone else who has just emerged from women's oldest and grandest profession, she could not bring herself to break the threads which held her to these two women—and to something beyond them which she would not realize. But after she was in bed, she could see in the darkness the church window in the sunset, and the altar rails, and the clergyman standing as he would do when Wilson and Laura were married.

So the three women lay in bed, thinking their own thoughts, with the sea moaning—moaning—as it broke in a long even wave and withdrew on the soft sand; quite a different sound every day, though Miss Ethel had heard it for fifty-six years. But she was scarcely conscious of hearing it at all, though it had formed an accompaniment to every thought and action of her life during all those years.

But to-night—perhaps because it was so warm and still, and she had the window facing the sea wide open—she did really listen to the waves; and that sound might perhaps have comforted her, with its deep note of unhasting permanence, if the ears of her mind had also been open to hear. But she only felt its melancholy. It seemed to accentuate her forlorn sense of having nothing stationary to hold on to, not even an unchanging God.

Chapter XI
The Gala

The Thorhaven season had passed its height, and that August month, towards which all the efforts of the lodging-house keepers and tradespeople converged during the year, was nearly at an end, while on every fence and wall employed for bill sticking could be read in large letters: "A Great Gala Night will take place on Thursday, August the twenty-ninth. Splendid Illuminations. Continental Attractions. Dancing on the Green from eight to ten-thirty."

The term Continental Attractions was the inspiration of Mr. Graham, who had recently visited the South of France on account of his wife's health—at least he gave that as his reason, though Mrs. Graham told all her friends confidentially that she would never have incurred so much trouble and expense if her husband had not shown symptoms of incipient bronchitis—and she equally believed herself to be speaking the truth. Anyway, there it was; and from the visit to Cannes resulted this idea of imparting a *joie de vivre* to the Thorhaven Gala by means of paper streamers and air balloons. There had been some consideration of squeakers and false noses; but one or two members of the Promenade Sub-Committee raised the reasonable objection that the squeakers would interfere with the band, while the false noses—— Well, there was something indefinably loose about false noses which they could feel but could not describe in words. At any rate, they were not going to allow such things on their promenade.

There was a good deal of talk concerning the Gala in the town; so that those inhabitants who were familiar with illustrated magazines and the lighter drama—and also possessed a sanguine temperament—no doubt went about picturing to themselves a still night with coloured lanterns hanging motionless against a deep blue sky, while a crowd of exuberant visitors disported themselves in pale garments and unusual attitudes for the amusement of the Thorhaven people.

But the clerk of the weather was not going to have anything so incongruous as all that, and the 29th rose cold and grey—one of those summer days which are a premonition of autumn. A strongish wind blew from the west; leaves came whirling down on the road leading to the promenade, and the sky was grey-black with clouds scudding across; while beneath it, a rising sea showed a line of white breakers in the gloom—like the cruel teeth of a monster seeking something to devour.

Still the evening came with no sign of rain; the band stationed at the edge of the green played cheerful dances with a will, and it was no fault of theirs that the music sounded so lost and futile amid the roaring of the sea— rather as if a penny whistle were to be played in a cathedral while the organ was booming out solemn music among the springing arches. Perhaps the visitors and the Thorhaven people felt something of this themselves, for they put no real zest into their attempts at carnival, but they danced rather grimly in the cold wind, with little tussocks in the grass catching their toes and the fairy lamps which edged the lawn blowing out one after the other.

At the windiest corner, near the hall, was planted the respectable middle-aged woman who sometimes assisted in cleaning the church—though she was herself an ardent Primitive—and in her arms she held a struggling mass of air balloons which seemed most anxious to escape over the North Sea to those parts of Europe where carnival is more at home. But no one seemed to be buying from her excepting a few children, whose needs were soon satisfied. Then a worn-looking young man came up and purchased two balloons for his children at home, but after that the woman stood there alone again, with the balloons buffeting about her head.

At another point farther down the promenade, a boy suffering from a slight cold in his head offered for sale a tray of those snake-like paper missiles which can be shot out suddenly with startling effect. But he seemed rather ashamed of his job and kept in the gloom as much as possible, now and then making a sale among the children, who ran in and out behind the more sheltered seats where their elders sat in winter coats.

Mr. Graham—as the originator of these attractions—felt exceedingly impatient, both with his fellow-townspeople and the visitors, as he sat watching. A chill air blew down the back of his neck and he was conscious of an incipient cold, which all added to his feeling of bitterness. "No earthly use trying!" he burst forth, rising abruptly from his seat. "English people don't know how to enjoy themselves, and it's no use trying to teach them."

He scowled first at the scene before him and then at his wife, who sat with Mrs. Bradford and Miss Ethel on a long wooden seat.

"You couldn't imagine the weather would be like this, dear," said Mrs. Graham soothingly.

"The air will do us good," added Miss Ethel, a little pink about the nose, but wishful to be polite.

"Well, there's plenty of it," he said bitterly, grabbing his hat, which threatened to blow away.

It was plain that he jested with an anxious heart, thinking of what might be said of his venture at the next Council meeting. Those very offensive fellows who always were against him would, of course, make capital out of this.... Suddenly he braced himself up and strode away across the lawn. They *should* frisk, if any influence of his could make 'em!

His wife looked after him sympathetically, then turned to Miss Ethel. "That's right!" she said. "Arthur will soon put a little more spirit into them. You see he knows how it is done. I shall never forget the way he entered into the spirit of the thing that time when we were abroad. If you could have seen him going down the Plage with a sort of a rattle in his hand and his hat on one side—— But there's something in the climate, of course."

"I suppose there must be," said Miss Ethel, with an involuntary glance at the couples jigging solemnly about the grass in front of her.

They sat silent for a time, feeling colder and colder, but sparing Mrs. Graham's feeling by remaining where they were. "Isn't that Caroline?" said Mrs. Bradford, after a long pause.

"I dare say. She told me the arrangements were somewhat different this evening, and she was to come off duty at half-past nine," said Miss Ethel.

Then Mr. Graham came back and bumped himself down so heavily on the wooden seat that the ladies felt a slight jar.

"No life!" he exclaimed. "No gaiety! No *joie de vivre!*" He paused, blowing his nose. "Well, this is the last time. I'll never attempt anything of the sort again."

"You must not say that. I am sure the Thorhaven people are grateful," murmured Miss Ethel.

"Old fool!" blurted out Mr. Graham with alarming ferocity and suddenness. "A woman like that ought to be kept indoors when other people are enjoying themselves, and only taken out in a churchyard on a chain. Fit for nothing else!"

"Arthur! What are you talking about?" said his wife, naturally startled.

"Well," he said, then had to swallow and choke. "Well, I bought one of those paper snakes just to encourage the lad and set things going a bit. Then I let it run out as I passed a dull-looking group that seemed not to be enjoying themselves. And—and——"

"Well, Arthur?"

"A wretched woman turned round and called me an impudent old scoundrel—told me she didn't want any grey-haired married men after her girls."

"I don't believe it! I can't! She meant somebody else. Don't you feel sure she must have meant her remark for some other passer-by, Mrs. Bradford?" said Mrs. Graham, much agitated by his annoyance.

Mrs. Bradford eyed Mr. Graham with stolid thoroughness. "I think she must. He doesn't look at all like that. But my husband used to say that the sedate middle-aged-looking ones were often the worst, so perhaps she may have thought the same."

"If she did, she was an idiot," said Mrs. Graham; then abruptly changed the subject. "Oh, there's Godfrey Wilson! I suppose he often comes through here on his way to his rooms."

"Yes, that's it. No fear of his wanting to dance with the girls on the promenade nowadays," answered Mr. Graham, beginning to recover himself by degrees. "Well, Lizzie, I think we've had enough of this, don't you? Shall we go in and have a bit of supper? Then I will see Mrs. Bradford and Miss Ethel home."

But as they walked away, he could not refrain from casting a backward glance at the decent woman struggling with her unruly air-balloons, and a sense of disappointed *joie de vivre* came over him once more. "I wish to goodness the whole bag o' tricks would blow away into the sea," he said. "I'd willingly pay the piper. I'm sick to death of seeing the things bob up and down in the wind."

"Are you?" said Miss Ethel in her sharp way. "Then why don't you buy them all up and send them to the children at the Convalescent Home that Laura is so interested in?"

"Now that's an idea," said Mr. Graham at once. For the feeling that it was his duty to give to a charitable institution when he could, had been handed down to him—it was a part of life, no less natural than having his hair cut or going to the dentist's. Out in the new, changed world this instinctive generosity might already be taking flight—scared away, as the fairies had been by steam traffic—but in Thorhaven it still remained.

So he went back to the woman selling air-balloons with restored self-satisfaction, and stood there in the high wind, diving into his pockets for the amount required. The air balloons blew about—purple, pink and white—all looking almost equally colourless by the faint light as they bobbed about the woman's head, impeding her view of the purchaser. A few moments later she was making her way home, thankful to be done with a job which seemed to her ridiculous.

Chapter XII
The End of the Gala

Godfrey Wilson waited until Mr. Graham had departed, then strolled slowly along the promenade towards Caroline. He had no real objection to anyone knowing that he spoke to her, but preferred to say a necessary word or two about the type-writing machine when Miss Ethel and her party were not there. This is what he told himself as he went along the path to the place where she stood with another girl, watching the dancing.

All the same it was something deeper than argument which informed his movements—something stronger than common sense. It was a stirring of the insatiable curiosity of the human being who has begun to be sexually interested in another. Though not exactly coarse-fibred, he was so far removed from anything attenuated as almost to be so. He only thought of himself.

He wanted to know what she was thinking of him, whether she liked him more or less than when they last met. And yet in spite of that he believed himself to be quite honest when he assured his conscience that he only wanted to say something about a paper carrier which had not worked well. For instinct is such a wonderful hand at camouflage that he believed quite honestly—despite previous experience—that he wanted nothing more. For the most wonderful thing about this kind of deception is that the same old trick may seem new time after time. Just as a healthy woman forgets what she has gone through on having her child, so a very virile man will forget—in a way—what he has experienced in pursuit of a girl.

At any rate, Godfrey Wilson was not at all conscious of going over old ground; though when he approached Caroline saying rather formally, "Good evening, Miss Raby. I just wanted to ask you if that paper carrier was working satisfactorily now——" he could not quite ignore the suggestion of a giggle in the attitude of Caroline's companion, who moved away at once with some murmur about finding a cousin. The "Two's company and three's none!" in her tone spoke as plainly as that. Wilson felt annoyed by it.

"Oh well, that was all I wanted to know," he said when she had given the information, and he spoke rather loudly and distinctly, so that anyone near might hear.

But as Caroline at once moved away to follow her friend, he suddenly felt that he wanted to say something more.

"The Gala has not been a very gay affair, has it? Nearly over now, though," he said.

She stood still again and they both glanced up and down the long promenade, which was fast emptying: just then a heavy cloud sailed across the moon, obscuring everything but those islands of light near the gas-lamps. The little coloured globes were by now more than half blown out, while the rest flickered uncertainly, accentuating the windy darkness. It was the last dance, and the band played very quickly. The few couples left were mostly men and girls more or less in love with each other who wanted to spin out the happy hours.

"Come!" said Wilson, putting his arm round Caroline's waist, on the impulse of the moment. "Let's dance these last few bars. It is all over."

All over—— It was curious how the words echoed in his own mind as he circled round faster and faster. He would not be dancing with little girls on the Thorhaven promenade any more after to-night. He would be a married man when the next Gala took place—ranged, respected; and though he felt a deep affection for Laura, he knew it was not on that altar alone that he had sacrificed his freedom. His wife's fortune would also just lift him above the dead-level where opportunities are very few, into the region where a clever and enterprising man with ambition is certain to find many; but he was sufficiently fond of Laura to make the prospect of matrimony with her agreeable, though he was not what is called a marrying man.

But a bridegroom of his type is bound to have regrets, unless in the thrall of an engrossing passion; and to-night Wilson felt these misgivings more acutely than he had done since his engagement—perhaps because the loss of bachelor freedom was getting so near. Therefore his dance with Caroline—though such a trivial matter in itself—was not simply a dance, but a last fling: and he felt a ridiculous desire to call out to the band to go on when he heard them stopping, so as to prolong something in his own life which he knew to be nearly at an end.

He did not do so, of course; and the performers at once began to pack up, thankfully looking forward to warmth and bed. Wilson and Caroline chanced to stop dancing near the turnstile leading on to the cliff, so they went out that way, which was near his lodgings, and equally convenient for her to reach the Cottage. One or two couples passed out just before them, but Caroline and Wilson were the last, and when they stepped into the clayey ground at the beginning of the cliff path, they seemed to plunge all at once into absolute darkness.

"Careful!" cried Wilson sharply. "You'll be over the cliff in a minute, if you don't look out." And he put his hand through her arm.

The sea gleamed very faintly under the black sky as they turned their backs on it and walked cautiously along the uneven path leading to the main road. At the corner she stood still and withdrew her arm. "I can manage all right now. It was so dark under the shadow of that wall. Good night."

"Oh no. I can't let you go home alone. You would be walking into a fence or spraining your ankle over a stone heap before you got to the Cottage," he answered. "Come on." And he took her arm again. "There! You see you are stumbling already."

She had trodden carelessly, disturbed by his touch, and she felt his grasp strengthen—then felt some instinct in herself fighting against it. "No. I'll go alone. I can quite well. I'd rather. I hate bringing you so far out of your way." She spoke in short phrases, nervously.

"Of course, I can't let you walk home by yourself in this," he said, his assurance somehow increased by her fluttering nervousness. "Don't be a silly girl. What are a few hundred yards to me one way or another?"

"Oh well!" Caroline suddenly gave way, feeling she had been making ridiculously too much of it. "Must be after eleven," she murmured. "The Committee extended the time to eleven. I expect they'll wish they hadn't, when it was such a cold night."

"I suppose they've been out after eleven before." But she knew by his tone he was not thinking of what he was saying. All that they had really to say to each other seemed to be passing through the electric current which passed between his strong, warm fingers and the tingling flesh of her arm—though they actually did discourse about Mr. Graham, and the balloons, and the financial disappointment which the Gala must have been to the Committee.

But near the gate of the Cottage Caroline resolutely withdrew her arm. "Please don't come up the drive. I'd rather you didn't. Good night!" She spoke in a low voice, hurriedly.

"Sure you're all right?" he said.

"Yes. Yes. Good night," she repeated.

He let her go a few steps, then she suddenly felt an arm of iron about her, the brief touch of his lips on her cheek—heard his voice saying with a queer accent of triumph: "I knew it would be like that!"

He was gone, leaving her standing there. He had satisfied the urge of a burning curiosity which had assailed him first as she sat in the window of Laura's drawing-room, and he noticed the magnolia texture of her healthy pallor and the little golden powdering of freckles on her nose. He had fought against that recollection. He had been ashamed to have begun it there. Now as he strode away into the dark he swore to himself that he was satisfied; he would never let himself go again; that he would be faithful to Laura in thought and deed.

As for Caroline—well, he remembered that she had walked out with a young man named Wilf; probably with others before that. A kiss more or less was not a serious thing to a girl of that sort; though he felt sorry, all the same, that he had been betrayed into giving it.

Caroline made her way up the dark drive, and on reaching the door she felt in her coat pocket for the latch-key. It was not there. Then she sought hastily in her other pocket and could not find it. Evidently she had dropped it on the road somewhere, but no one could see a small article like that now, even if it lay on the pathway.

Well, there was nothing for it but to knock at the door. She looked up at the house which loomed above her, a dark block with faintly gleaming windows, and the thud, thud, made by her knuckles seemed extraordinarily loud. But the stillness which followed seemed intense—seemed only to be accentuated by the heavy sound of the sea which she never consciously heard in the daytime, any more than Miss Ethel or the other Thorhaven people.

After a while she knocked again, but the house still lay quiet—with the peculiar deadness about it of houses seen from the outside when those within are all asleep. In the room just above the front door Miss Ethel was deep in the first stupid slumber of exhaustion produced by a long day's work and the evening walk in a high wind. She was so tired that she had ceased some time ago to lie awake and listen for Caroline coming in, though she felt it was her duty to do so. But nearly every night now she went to bed early and lay like a log, not caring about anything more until the morning. If the world came to an end, she must go to bed—she could no more.

Caroline down below stood hesitating whether to throw a stone up or not, but remembered that Mrs. Bradford was so timid that she always covered up her ears with the blanket for fear of hearing burglars in the night—priding herself indeed on this timidity, and telling people that when you once had had a husband you lost your nerve for sleeping alone. So

Caroline knew there was no help to be had in that quarter, and yet she did not like to startle Miss Ethel after that fall among the half-built houses which had been more than an ordinary faint, though no one made anything of it.

However, she knocked again on the door, blows that seemed to echo through the whole of Thorhaven. She glanced nervously over her shoulder, picturing the male inhabitants of Emerald Avenue and Cornelian Crescent and Sapphire Terrace, hastily flinging on trousers and boots to see what the matter was, while their wives made shrill-voiced ejaculations from the bed. She saw it all quite plainly on the darkness as the noise reverberated through the still night. Suddenly she lost her nerve. That kiss at the gate still hovered in the back of her consciousness, waiting for a fuller realization; but it had left her fluttering and tingling with emotion, so that she was less mistress of herself than usual.

Not that she had not been kissed before, and by others besides Wilf; but it had never been like this, because now for the first time a kiss woke a response which bewildered her. She began to cry.

Then she tried to pull herself together. After all, it could not be very late. What an idiot to be standing there crying, when Aunt Creddle lived only a ten minutes' walk away! Of course she could go and stay the night there. Very likely Aunt Creddle might be still up, for she took in washing for one or two people, and sometimes did the ironing after the children were in bed——

Caroline gave a sob of relief as she got to this, and turning her back on the house she began to run stumbling down the drive. When she reached the open road and was free from the heavy shadow of the privet hedge, she felt her self-confidence gradually coming back to her.

All the houses in Emerald Avenue were in darkness, but on nearing the Creddles she saw a little glimmer of light through the glass pane of the front door. It was as she had hoped, for in response to her knock, Mrs. Creddle herself unchained the door and peered out into the dark. "Is that somebody from Mrs. White's?" she asked. "I thought she wasn't expecting until next week at the——" The good woman broke off suddenly and her voice went up several notes: "You, Caroline!"

"Yes. I lost my latch-key and I can't make them hear. I was afraid I should startle Miss Ethel if I threw anything up at her window," said Caroline, speaking quickly. "I didn't know if it might give her a turn, after that fall of hers. And you can't waken Mrs. Bradford. She wraps her head up in her petticoat and sleeps like the dead."

"Well, it's a lucky thing I happened to be up finishing the ironing," said Mrs. Creddle. "Your uncle wouldn't have liked it if you'd come hammering at our door and letting the whole street know you were locked out."

"I didn't lose the key on purpose," said Caroline rather sullenly, as she followed her aunt into the warm, light kitchen. "I couldn't help it."

"What made you so late in?" said Mrs. Creddle. "Here, sit you down and I'll get you a drink of cocoa. Girls never used to be having latch-keys and careering about at all hours in my day."

"But it isn't your day now, thank goodness!" said Caroline, who was feeling excited and irritable. "I had a dance on the green after I came off duty, that was all."

"Prom's been closed a long time," said Mrs. Creddle. "I heard the next-door folks come back. But we was all young once, and I dare say you and Wilf have been kissing and making friends again on the way home. Is that it?"

For some obscure reason this question angered Caroline almost beyond bearing.

"I told you I'd done with Wilf, and I have," she said rather hysterically. "I wouldn't let him kiss me now for anything on earth. I don't know how I ever could fancy him. I——"

"Hush!" said Mrs. Creddle, glancing towards the stairs. "There's your uncle moving. I'm afraid he won't be best pleased to see you here, Carrie. And he would have pickle for his tea, though I told him not, so he's a bit fretty to start with."

Before she had finished speaking Mr. Creddle was upon them, hastily dressed in night-shirt and trousers. "Now, what's all this?" he said, and his tone certainly did betray the effect of cheap vinegar on a weak digestion.

So Mrs. Creddle explained matters while Caroline stood listening.

"Who came home with you?" said Creddle, turning with a dark face towards the two women. "I saw the bills. Dancing was over a good bit since. Who brought you home?"

"That's my business," she answered, pale and obstinate.

"Is it? Well, it's my business to take you back to your place," he said. Then he went on, raising his voice: "Do you think I'm going to have a niece of mine—that I've brought up like my own—stopping out all night? The lasses in my family and in your aunt's family, too, have always been respectable—and you will be an' all, so long as I have anything to do with you."

"I'm not going back to the Cottage to-night, though. I'm going to stop here and sleep on the sofa," said Caroline defiantly.

"Hush, Carrie," pleaded Mrs. Creddle anxiously. "That isn't the way to speak to your uncle, you know. He only means it for your good."

Mr. Creddle reached for his boots. "I won't have her stop out all night," he repeated. "What would your mother ha' thought if you'd done such a thing when you were in service?"

"Only I *aren't* in service like aunt was," answered Caroline, getting excited again. "Things are quite different from what they used to be then. You can't judge by what went on when you were young, can he, aunt?"

But Mrs. Creddle only shook her head; for somehow those words "stopped out all night" came echoing on from her youth and she felt the force of tradition at this moment no less than her husband. Always that phrase had conveyed something derogatory concerning the girl about whom it was used; and never would she or her sister Ellen have earned it while they were in service for any earthly consideration. She was still faithful to all the traditions of that skilled trade to which she had served a long apprenticeship, and which is one of the most intricate and difficult in the world. For a mass of oral knowledge handed down from one to another—accuracy, intelligence, self-control, a very high standard of personal chastity—these things formed only a part of the equipment of Caroline's aunts when they were young, and such girls as they formed an unorganized guild of service which can never be excelled in England, whatever comes. They were the best maid-servants in the world, and they did not know it. But they had a great pride in themselves, if not in their fine calling, and Mrs. Creddle felt this stir within her as she listened to her husband.

"Your uncle's right," she said. "Maybe other people will get to know you lost your key, and they mightn't believe you. You wouldn't like it to get about that you'd stopped out all night."

"I shouldn't care. I know I've done nothing wrong," said Caroline, beginning to take off her hat.

"Now, my lass!" said Creddle grimly, as he finished lacing his boots, "you're coming with me. Don't let's have no nonsense!"

"I tell you, I'm not coming," said Caroline, pale about the lips and trembling a little.

"Come! Come! Carrie," said Mrs. Creddle, beginning to cry. "Don't anger your uncle. He's that wore out he didn't know where to put himself when he got home to-night, and yet here he is with his boots on ready to take you back to your place. And he's always treated you like his own, and so have I, so far as I know how. Many's the little treat we've gone without, and never grudged it, so as to bring you up nice; and this is how you pay us back."

"Oh, aunt, I know you have," said Caroline, and her eyes filled, though they had been hard and dry a minute before. "I do know how good you and uncle have been. Only I won't be taken back as if I were a little trapesing general that had been misbehaving herself. I can't!"

"There's no talk of misbehaving," said Creddle. "And I aren't going to have any. You get your hat on and come with me."

Caroline's face stiffened; then she felt the touch of Mrs. Creddle's roughened, kind hand on her arm, and saw that jolly face puckered with crying which had smiled a welcome on her all her life. She gave a great gulp and walked to the door, Creddle following her.

For she belonged—poor Caroline—to the company of those who can really love, and they are always liable to give way suddenly when fighting those they love, because they cannot bear to see the pain.

Chapter XIII
Next Morning

Miss Ethel came into the kitchen as Caroline finished washing up the breakfast things. There was a constrained atmosphere about both of them which seemed even to affect the small fire which burnt sulkily in the grate, but nothing was said concerning the events of the previous night.

"Oh! Caroline, I wonder if you would kindly take a message for me to Miss Temple on your way to the promenade?" said Miss Ethel, rather stiffly.

But on the whole the affair of the previous night had been less odious than Caroline had feared. Still it had been rather like an ugly nightmare, all the same—Uncle Creddle banging on the door until one startled woman opened it while the other peered over the banisters. They had thanked Mr. Creddle, saying Caroline ought to be more careful: and Mrs. Bradford added that some burglar had no doubt picked up the key and would come and murder them in their beds. But there the matter ended.

Now, however, with the mention of Laura's name, the recollection of that kiss at the gate last night sprang up from some deep place within Caroline's consciousness and overwhelmed everything else. She could not go to Laura's door and perhaps be obliged to answer kind words and pleasant looks; she could not do it. "I'm sorry, Miss Ethel," she muttered, bending over the washing-bowl, "but there's not time."

Miss Ethel glanced at the clock and saw that there was time; but she could not insist, and so thought it more dignified to go away without making any remark. Still she felt irritated to an unreasonable degree, for her disturbed night had left her tired and nervous.

A few minutes later Caroline went out. There had been a change in the wind, which now blew lustily from the north-east, and the sun was shining. As she came down the street leading to the promenade, the surface of her mind responded to the pricking liveliness of the salt air and the sight of the open sea in front of her. A heavy rain towards dawn had washed down mud from the cliffs which the high tide had carried away, so now the water was a milky dun-colour, scattered with millions of opal lights, answering more closely just then to the thought of a jewelled sea than even the sparkling sapphire Mediterranean.

A middle-aged visitor who had passed constantly in and out through the barrier and knew Caroline by sight, gave her a sprightly "Good morning" as he went through. "Most invigorating! Most invigorating!"

"Yes. Makes you feel as if you could jump over the moon, doesn't it?" said Caroline gaily—that surface mind responding to his brisk jollity.

"Ha! Ha! So long as you haven't a liver to weigh you down," jested the rosy-faced gentleman. Then he stepped away down the promenade, well pleased with himself and his surroundings, and feeling that he was not such an old dog yet, so long as he could enjoy a joke with a girl on the promenade.

Caroline looked after him with a smile which gradually faded from her lips as the slight stimulation from without ceased to act. For beneath it all there was something inside, deep down within her, which was not to be touched by the influences of sea air or sunshine—something that watched anxiously and doggedly for one thing and would heed no other.

But the people came and went—came and went—until her knee ached with the clutch and her whole being with watching.... And still the one man she was looking for never put his broad-palmed, long-fingered hand on the iron bar or turned his heavy-featured face towards her little window.

She kept telling herself that she was tired after last night, so as to explain the ache, but her little, pale face was looking pinched in the light from the sea when Laura Temple paused at the barrier to say a few words. The two girls spoke to each other through the little window; one smiling, the other rather grave and reluctant. They talked a moment or two of trivial things— the weather, the Gala—but Caroline felt a queer animosity towards this pleasant, kind girl whose lover had kissed her the night before. Though she told her surface self that the kiss was only a "bit of fun" and meant nothing, that other self knew well enough that it had meant quite enough to constitute an injury to a bride who was to be married in less than three weeks' time.

She replied abruptly, turning over the leaves of her account book; irritated by this contradictory sense of being obliged to feel she had done an injury when she knew she really had not. So at last Laura thought she had a headache or something, and soon went on towards the Cottage.

Miss Ethel came to the door, and at once took Laura into the living-room. Mrs. Bradford sat as usual on an arm-chair, idle with a clear conscience, because of her great, successful effort in the past.

Laura greeted them both gaily, for she felt the world was an agreeable place that morning. "I received your message with an almond cake from the baker's. I do hope your news is something good, too," she said.

But Miss Ethel did not respond to the mild pleasantry. "Yes. I had to get the baker's boy to take a message, because I am not very well to-day, and Caroline declined to call round on her way to the promenade."

"Said she hadn't time," added Mrs. Bradford. "She had quite sufficient time. And considering that she came in at all hours last night after pretending to lose the latch-key, I think she might have done what Ethel asked. No doubt she had been wandering about with some man. She went to the Creddles, intending to stay the night there, but Creddle brought her back."

"Oh, I feel sure she really did lose the key," said Laura. "It is a thing I have done myself before now. And I'm sure I never wandered about at night with young men."

"But she pretended that she had been here earlier and was unable to make anyone hear. I didn't like that. We are not Rip van Winkles," said Miss Ethel crisply.

Laura laughed, anxious to conciliate them both for Caroline's sake. "I dare say she was afraid of disturbing you. She is a kind-hearted girl, I am sure, and she would remember that you have been ill, Miss Ethel."

"And yet she declined to go on a simple errand for me this morning," said Miss Ethel. "No, they are all alike: all for self. The young people of the present day think of nothing but their own amusement."

She paused and added, anxious to be just, "Though I must own that Caroline was kind when I was ill. I dare say there is something good-hearted about her, at the bottom: but it is her general attitude which I so dislike."

"If we only had Ellen back!" moaned Mrs. Bradford from the depths of the arm-chair. "Or somebody like Ellen."

"You may just as well wish for butter at fourteen-pence a pound or oranges twelve a penny like we used to get in Flodmouth Market," retorted Miss Ethel. Then her voice changed, taking on a heavy, inward note. "Those days are done. They'll never come back any more."

"I mean," said Mrs. Bradford, who had all the curiosity often shown by stupid people, "what sort of a young man Caroline has got now. A great deal depends on that." And she looked inquiringly at Laura.

"I'm sure I don't know," said Laura. "Caroline's young men are her affair, not mine."

"At any rate," said Miss Ethel, "we have not brought you here on a busy morning to talk about them. We know you must have a great deal on your hands just now, preparing for the wedding."

"Oh, it makes a great difference, having no house to get ready," said Laura, flushing at the mention of her wedding, as she could not help doing, though she felt such a sign of emotion to be ridiculous at this time of day. "We must stay in my cottage until the house Godfrey has taken is at liberty, and they say that won't be before the end of March at the earliest."

"I don't think I should have liked that," said Mrs. Bradford. "I remember how my dear husband insisted on having everything absolutely complete, down to the very toilet-tidies on the looking-glasses, before he took me home as a bride. But there are few like him." And she sighed and glanced up at the quite imposing photograph which she had long since come to believe exactly resembled Mr. Bradford in life.

Laura felt a very little annoyed for the moment, being sensitive on this point of a house because hints had not failed to reach her that Godfrey was considered to be feathering his nest at her expense; but the next minute she forgot her annoyance in a tender flow of sympathy for this other woman who had lost everything which she herself was about to possess.

"Godfrey and I thought it preferable to waiting until the spring," she said gently. "But of course I should have liked my new home to be all ready for me, as yours was."

"Well, you needn't regret the toilet-tidies," said Miss Ethel. "Green paper with magenta ribbon, if I remember right." Then she paused a moment, nervously trying to steel herself for an effort which was exceedingly painful to her. "But what we asked you to come in for was this——" She paused again to clear her throat. "We have decided to sell this house, and we thought you would kindly convey the message to Godfrey for us."

"Of course I will," said Laura readily. The question as to why a letter could not have been sent to Godfrey was latent in her tone, but Miss Ethel did not answer it, because she herself did not know how she dreaded the effort of writing the letter.

"We knew you would be seeing Godfrey this afternoon—we thought perhaps you would break it to him."

"We have only just decided," added Mrs. Bradford. "But I daresay we shall be all right in Emerald Avenue. There is a pleasant window in the front bedroom facing south. So long as I have my knitting and a warm corner I can make myself happy. My dear husband once said that my disposition made me immune from the arrows of adversity. It was a beautiful thing to say, and I have never forgotten it."

"I'll be sure to tell Godfrey," said Laura, for once bluntly disregarding Mrs. Bradford's reminiscences, because she understood far more than they thought. It was plain enough that Miss Ethel had sent in this haste so as to make the matter irrevocable—to strengthen a decision almost beyond her powers. But once they had talked openly about leaving the house, it became an established thing.

"Tell Godfrey we can be out by Christmas, if he is able to effect a sale," said Miss Ethel. "We must leave the roses, of course, as there will be no garden in Emerald Avenue. The privet hedge has been clipped this year, but it will want pruning in January."

"Oh, Miss Ethel!" said Laura, with a catch in her throat, suddenly feeling the tears running down, though she had no thought of crying a moment earlier.

For Miss Ethel, as she stood there very erect, talking in that dry, clear tone, with her thin face towards the light and the right temple twitching a little, looking out at the garden she had loved to tend, was a sight very touching to a sensitive heart. And though Laura knew that it was not such a terrible misfortune to leave an agreeable house with a nice garden for a smaller one less pleasant, she still felt—ridiculous though her reason knew it to be—that the atmosphere of the low room was charged with something momentous. The throb! throb! throb! of a heavy sea at low tide came through the window, and it sounded to Laura's excited perceptions like the tread of something dreadful coming. Perhaps she was in a state of heightened emotion owing to her nearly approaching marriage, and that made her unduly impressionable, but she did experience a queer, helpless sense of destiny approaching such as you feel in dreams.

But Miss Ethel had conquered a momentary trembling of the lips caused by Laura's tears, and she crisply broke the silence. "I dare say you think we are making a mountain out of a molehill."

"No, no," said Laura eagerly. "Only you will have less work to do, and by next year at this time you may be really glad you are not here."

"Shall I?" said Miss Ethel. "I hope it may be so!"

"Don't take it like that, Miss Ethel!" said Laura in a quick, sharp tone, most unusual for her. "Things can never be as they were again. Is it likely? Look out into the world. There's not a corner where you don't feel the backwash of a storm of some sort. You and I have lived in such a sheltered happy way here that we don't realize what's going on unless we are brought up against it by something in our own lives." She wanted to be kind—yet words which were not very kind came out in spite of herself: and she felt herself trembling a little, as if they had to do with a deep emotion of her own which it distressed her to bring to light. "You can't feel sure of anything or anybody in the whole world. Anybody may change. They can't help it, any more than you can help seeing it." She was very pale now, aghast at what had grown from a faint stirring of unformulated doubt to a spoken reality. Almost every sensitive person has trembled thus before something which has sprung up into sight through the accidental touching of a hidden spot in the mind.

But that only lasted a moment—the next, she was not going to leave it so. Every particle of her being rebelled against what she had seen and she would rather doubt her senses than her love. "I except Godfrey, of course," she said, lifting up her head with a little laugh. "*He* remains stable."

"Yes. Yes. Of course," responded Miss Ethel absently, her mind so full of what they had just decided to do that she could think of nothing else. "Then you will tell Godfrey? I don't think there is any need for me to write."

"He will come in to see you, no doubt." Laura had remained standing since that moment when she rose hastily from her seat, and she went forward now with a gesture which showed she did not intend to sit down again. "I have such heaps to do this morning. I'm afraid I must run away now."

But as she touched Miss Ethel's hand with her own she was startled by its icy coldness. In a moment her sympathy flowed back again over those dreadful thoughts, washing them away. "I know you'll love your new home when you get settled, and you will have all your friends just the same. More, because you will be nearer the town." And she pressed her lips to that white cheek.

Miss Ethel did not seem to relax in that embrace, or to be in the least sensible of the natural kindness which permeated every fibre of Laura's being like the sweetness of sun-warmed fruit, but perhaps she did feel a little comforted by that soft human contact all the same.

For she went with the guest to the door and stood alone there watching until the sound of steps and the click of the gate gave place to silence. The builders had gone away for their dinner-hour, and the close-shaven grass in the sunshine near the high hedge seemed so cloistered—so much more remote than it really was. Before those new houses came, you need not see anything beyond the privet hedge unless you wished—— But now the outside was close upon her. It was time to give in and go away.

As she stood there with the neat curled hair over her forehead blowing in the wind, and her short skirt and blouse trimly set about her spare figure, she was thinking thoughts which were almost incredibly different from what she looked—seeking all over the world with a sort of desperate forlornness for a corner where her mind could find rest.

Then the very quiet of the half-built houses over the hedge reminded her that she must go in to fry the rissoles for the midday dinner, but she revolted from the anticipated smell of hot fat with a sensation of physical sickness. For she had never possessed a robust appetite, and until this last year had scarcely ever sat down to a meal prepared by herself: so she did not bring to the task that interest which a good appetite or a natural taste for cooking will give even to those who have had no previous experience.

However, it had to be done, so she went in, catching sight as she passed through the hall of a roll of music returned by Laura: but it failed to stir any regret that she was always too tired to practise nowadays. Leisure—which she had all her life regarded as a right, no more to be considered than water or air—was hers no longer.

But she had no idea that she was sharing the exact experience of thousands of women throughout England—throughout Europe: that as she stood there alone over a stove in a quiet little house in a remote part of Yorkshire, carrying out the everyday details of her narrow existence, she was more widely and actually international than the manual workers themselves.

She only knew that she loathed the smell of frying fat.

Chapter XIV
The Cliff Top

Caroline had just come back from her tea and stood at the door of the pay-box, talking to Lillie, who was about to go off duty. The bright light reflected from the sea shone on the two girls, and on some children with brown legs and streaming hair who raced along the promenade.

"Going for a walk?" said Caroline, glancing idly in front of her at the expanse of dappled water.

"No. Mother has a bad cold and we're full up with visitors. I shall go straight home."

Then—just at this least expected moment—the thing happened for which some hidden feeling within her had been so intently waiting all day. She saw Godfrey standing there as she had pictured, with his broad, long-fingered hand on the iron bar; the hand so indicative—had she but known—of the contradictions in his character.

Lillie sat down again to release the clutch, and he passed through to the promenade. "Oh, lovely afternoon, isn't it?" he said, and walked briskly away between the neat rows of bedding plants.

The two girls looked after him; at last Lillie said with a slight giggle: "Seems in a hurry, doesn't he? But I expect he's got his young lady waiting for him. My word, she'd give him beans if she knew he saw you home last night, wouldn't she?" A pause, during which Caroline failed to respond; then, rather shortly: "Well, so long!" But Caroline did not notice; her whole mind bent on Godfrey's retreating figure as it went firmly down the broad concrete walk of the promenade—for now the question she'd been craving to ask all day had been answered. He thought nothing about what happened last night. The kiss had been nothing to him. He intended to show her that he did not recognize any slightest claim on his attention which she might think she had gained from it.

Then she had to cease looking after him in order to answer a stout lady visitor who made a point of being nice to the girl at the pay-box. "Yes—a great pity the weather was not like this for the Gala."

But all the time she was saying to herself, with the queer, dazed feeling which comes from a sudden shock of discovery: "I'm gone on him! I'm fair gone on him, and him going to be married!"

Even in her thoughts she usually chose her words—just as she kept herself scrupulously "nice" underneath to match her carefully tended hands and well-brushed hair. But now she reverted back to the expressions of her earliest girlhood. "I only meant a bit of fun, and I'm fair gone on him."

Oh! it was desolating—most miserable. There was nothing on earth to be got from it but heartache. She had tried to do the best for herself, and Fate had treated her like this—stabbed her from behind. It was abominable that she should be punished so for a bit of fun when other girls got off scot-free who had done all sorts of things that she would be ashamed of doing. Life was unfair. It was horribly unfair——

An Urban District Councillor on his way home separated himself from the stream of men with bags which emerged blackly from the railway station and flowed over Thorhaven between half-past five and half-past six. "Fine evening! Fine evening!" he said, bustling through the barrier.

For a moment the agony lifted; but when he was gone it started again worse than ever—like the pain in an inflamed nerve. The waste of it! She had thrown away her best asset for nothing. She could no longer fall in love with the rich young man who might want to marry her one day—as she had always more or less sub-consciously expected—because she loved Godfrey. Instinct warned her that the best goods in her shop window were gone without any return, and for the moment her chief feeling was an intense anger against fate first and then against Godfrey.

Not that she blamed him particularly for the kiss. Any man would kiss a girl when he saw her home if he had a chance, of course. But she was vaguely furious with him because he was the cause of such a disorganization of all her life plans. She felt cheated, though she did not realize what she was cheated of, as she sat there looking out of her little window towards the north.

Through the remainder of the evening and all the next day her mood remained thus—indrawn and sombre. The people going on the promenade passed by her like marionettes, and she like another marionette responded, but there was no feeling in it at all. She might equally well have seen the whole lot of them, herself included, jerked by wires from a sardonic heaven that had no purpose, no plan—only such figures of thought were not within her scope; still the feeling was there, corroding her faith in life.

At last Saturday night came. But the week of long working hours during which she had been constantly in the sea air and yet protected from wind and rain, had left her filled with vitality, despite her bitterness of mind. The night was not dark, because of a growing moon and pale stars peppering the sky, and as she walked along the light road with no care for her footsteps she found a vent for that unusual vitality in a certain habit of her girlhood which she had almost entirely dropped during the past year or two. Often enough before that, she had walked about the Thorhaven streets imagining herself in all sorts of impossible situations, though always happy, beloved and rich. But she had since given it up, as she had put away her dolls a year or two earlier; and she now felt a secret shame in abandoning herself to it again—as if she had at fourteen taken to playing with dolls once more.

So she let herself imagine Godfrey walking by her side with his arm through hers— kissing her at the gate. After all, nobody would ever know. It hurt nobody; it was all she would ever get. Then weakened by her dreaming she actually did see Godfrey come forth from a clump of dark elders and had not the power to walk straight on as she would have done half an hour earlier. Instead, she stood still and looked at him—disturbed, unhappy, yet with the dull bitterness suddenly gone.

He was close to her before he spoke; then he said hurriedly: "I only wanted to apologize for the other night. I hope you were not offended?" But he knew quite well she was not: it was the urge of that curiosity still burning within him which drove him to find out what she had felt—how his kiss had left her—whether he had been able to reach anything in her.

"You didn't seem to be bothering much about me when you went through into the promenade," she said at last.

He was answered in part; the next moment she felt his arm through hers, just as she had been dreaming on the road, only the reality had a compelling magnetism which was beyond any dreams. "Let us go a little way along the cliff," he said. "I want to speak to you. I want to explain." He spoke excitedly, with a sort of jaded eagerness in his tone; and though she knew her own unwisdom, she went with him.

The turning towards the cliff was just beyond the Cottage, on the opposite side of the road, and consisted of a gravel path that opened out into a small space on the cliff top. It was a lonely spot, out of the way of strolling visitors at that time of night: the bench in the middle of the gravelled space lay empty in the luminous sea-twilight with a great arch of sky overhead and the waves below catching a gleam from moon and stars on every ripple. Though Thorhaven might not be beautiful on a Gala evening, with futile little lamps and starved visitors blown about by the wind, it had, on such nights as these, an exquisite, cool beauty which appealed to the spirit as well as the senses.

As they sat down, Caroline could feel his fingers trembling on her arm; suddenly his kiss struck hard on her lips and her head fell back so that he could see the dark rims of her eyelashes. "Ah! You're in it too—you're in it too," he murmured triumphantly—caring for nothing but that triumphant knowledge.

She knew what he meant—they were both in it. Their oneness enveloped her in a cloud of rapture. Then she jerked herself out of his embrace. "No. No. I can't have you kissing me. It isn't fair to take your fun out of me when you're going to be married directly. I don't know how you can want to do it."

He jumped up without speaking and walked towards the cliff edge. "Good God!" he burst out. "You don't imagine I *want* to be in love with you! I'm in hell—hell! Whatever I do, I see your face. It's beyond all reason——" He stopped short, amazed and enraged by this strange, biting curiosity which made him mad about a girl who was nothing—who was not even really pretty. What could influence men in this way—driving them to insane acts for the sake of some one woman out of all the millions? There must be something not yet understood. Suddenly he dropped on to the seat, holding his head in his hands. "I don't know what on earth I am going to do," he said.

She looked at him—so helpless in his passion—and the protective instinct of a real woman for her man began to stir in her: so, in spite of her own pain, she tried hard to find something to say that would comfort him. "You—you'll get over it," she said, her voice shaking. "It isn't as if you and I had been going together long, you know. You'll soon forget me."

"Don't!" he said sharply.

She drew back offended. "Oh! All right." She rose with a sort of dignity. "I think I'd better be going home. It must be getting late."

"Now you're vexed." He peered at her—haggard-eyed in that curious twilight from the sea. "Can't you see that everything you do and say makes me want you more? If you'd only turned out a fool!" He drew a long breath.

"I must be going home," she repeated, moving away.

He caught hold of her dress as she went. "Carrie, I can't let you go. I can't do without you."

"You'll have to," she said sombrely. "We shall both have to. There's no help for it."

He waited a moment, then the words seemed to come out of themselves—despite him. "I'm not married yet, you know."

She started. "You don't mean——" Then she backed away from him, the silhouette of her slim figure very clear against the luminous background of sea and sky—every line of it dragging at his senses—hurting him with pity. "You know you couldn't do it," she said after a pause. "We neither of us could. It would kill her. Besides, I couldn't sneak another girl's man after the banns were up and the cake bought—a girl who'd never done me any harm. I aren't so low down as all that, yet."

"Anything is better than marrying without love," he said, but he said it half-heartedly. How was a decent man to throw over a charming devoted girl to whom he was to be married in a fortnight, shaming her before all her little world after he had sought and won her? He thought of Laura's soft acquiescence with an agony of self-reproach and impatience. Then he heard Caroline speaking again, her voice low and clear with the murmur of the sea running in and out of it—he felt it go to his heart.

"It's too late to begin to think whether you'll be miserable or not now," she said. "You made her fond of you. It was your own doing. And you wouldn't get me if you did give her up. I'd no more take you from her, now she's got her wedding-dress and all, than I'd stick a knife into a baby sleeping in its pram. She worships you—can't you see that? It would spoil all her life."

"What about yours—and mine?" he said. "You don't really care for me, or you couldn't talk like that."

She looked away to the glimmering sea, not troubling to answer him. What was the use? He knew.

"Well, I'll be getting on," she said at last.

But he found the hopelessness in her voice unbearable.

"Carrie, we can't leave it like this," he said. "I can't do without you; that's a fact. We must arrange something." He hesitated. "You—you won't cease to be friends with me just because I'm married, will you?"

She moved so quickly out of the reach of his hand that she stood poised on the extreme edge of the cliff. "What do you mean?" she said fiercely. "Is that what you take me for? Then let me tell you I never carried on with a married man in my life and never shall. You're as good as married now. Leave me alone. You think you can talk to me like that because I'm fond of you. But before I'd have anything to do with those underhand ways, I'd jump over this cliff and have done with it. I would, too. I aren't *that* sort, you know—though I have behaved like a silly fool."

But her very defiance only gave his curiosity a keener edge, and he moved towards her with his hand outstretched. "You won't get out of it like that," he said. "Do you suppose I'm going to let you go now, and never see you alone again? I will see you, or I'll chuck the whole thing up to-morrow morning, come what may."

She glanced at him sideways, temporizing: "I shall be meeting you, no doubt."

But he was not to be deceived. "You mean you have done with me unless I break off my engagement. Very well. I'll do it."

She shook her head. "That's nonsense," she said sharply. "You know you can't do it."

"It is only what you did yourself," he said sullenly. "You threw over that young man I saw you with at the dance, and I don't suppose you considered it a crime."

They spoke as enemies, throwing the barbed words back and forth.

"Of course I didn't."

"But why not? It was the same thing."

"No; that was quite different," she said.

"I don't see it. Why different?"

"Because——" She struggled: but suddenly her voice began to tremble. "Oh, I didn't know what love was like then. But he never cared as Miss Laura does. And I shouldn't have minded so much about her, if I hadn't found out for myself——" She broke off. "Only three weeks from the wedding. You couldn't do it, either. Not when it came to only three weeks from the wedding, you couldn't. You know that as well as I do."

"But you always say everybody ought to do the best for themselves. I remember your saying so. What sense is there in spoiling our two lives for the sake of a third?" he said, eagerly and yet heavily. "Why can't you act up to what you believe in this instance, just as you did when you threw over that young man?"

She shook her head, looking at him through unshed tears. "I don't know," she said. "But when it comes to, you can't do it. You know you can't, either. If we were the weak sort, we might."

He let fall her hand which he had been holding and sat down heavily, almost with a groan, upon the wooden bench. It was true enough, what she said. They were both better than their word.

And yet it was not any hope of a future reward which sustained them as they sat there side by side, not touching each other, while the Flamborough lights swung out monotonously across the sea and the waves washed up with regular beat upon the shore. They imagined they believed this life to be probably all—and yet they did not seize what they could get and let everything else go. It was because love constrained them. They felt within themselves the stirring of their own immortality. But they experienced none of the exultation of sacrifice as they turned away from the cliff edge and walked silently, glumly, towards the high road, she trying to wipe the tears away with her fingers so that he should not notice.

As they neared the gate of the Cottage, Godfrey said suddenly: "You don't think I'm frightened of what people say?"

She shook her head. "I aren't so silly as that." She hesitated, then held out her hand. "It's good-bye, then." But her voice trembled again, though she tried to keep it steady, and the next minute she was in his arms, crying her heart out.

"Caroline! What are we to do? What are we to do?" he said, the tears hot in his own eyes. "I can't give you up. I can't live without you."

She clung to him, not answering, and his mind darted back to the name he had given her that first time he had his arm about her at the promenade dance. A nymph on fire. There was something just so fresh and cool about her in the midst of all her passion——

Then he felt her releasing herself gently, but with determination. "What's the use of beginning it all over again?" she said. "You know there's nothing to be done. I aren't that sort. And you aren't either. Don't you know she's got the bride-cake bought, poor girl?"

He could not speak. Her childish insistence on the wedding-cake having been purchased was like a knife through his heart. If only he had left her alone!

"I deserve to be shot for letting you in for this," he said hoarsely. Then he broke out again. "I can't stand it! I must break off my engagement— whatever it costs and however she suffers. You're suffering. And I am! Good God, I should think I am."

But he spoke the last word to empty air—and the next moment he could hear the click of the gate as she slipped away from him up the dark drive.

Chapter XV
The Cinema

On Monday evening Caroline stood at the corner of Emerald Avenue, not sure whether to go down it or not, for she had not visited the Creddles since Mr. Creddle so ignominiously took her back to the Cottage at midnight.

While she was hesitating a cab-load of sunburnt children, accompanied by a stout, jolly-looking mother, went by on their way to the railway station. It was the beginning of that exodus which would grow more general every day during the next fortnight until the season was over. Already cards had appeared in one or two windows, and those who had let their houses furnished for "August month" while they found shelter in tumble-down cottages, tents or converted railway carriages, were coming back—glad now the money was in their pockets that they had borne the discomfort, though each year on departing they said "Never again!" A sea-gull flew across the sky with the pink sunset on its outspread wings, and below, the grey church stood in a tender haze against a sheet of gold. But this peaceful time at the end of summer only increased Caroline's restlessness. There was nothing she wanted to do. She neither liked to walk alone, nor to find friends.

So she stood there listlessly, trying to make up her mind whether she should go to see Aunt Creddle or not; and as she did so a slim woman of about forty who had been very pretty came down the Avenue. Caroline remembered quite well what Mrs. Creddle had said about her. She had gone into an office as typist instead of being in service like the other sisters, and thought herself too fine for those who wanted her, but was not fine enough for those she wanted. So one sister married a farm labourer who became a prosperous farmer, the other did not disdain a chimney sweep, and both now possessed houses and children and warm places of their own in the world, while the prettiest still tripped with a rather over-bright smile about the Thorhaven streets, aware of really superior refinement, but not finding much comfort in it.

She stopped to speak to Caroline—and without knowing why, Caroline felt as if a cold wind out of the future had blown drearily across her mind.

"Waiting for Wilf?" asked the girl, smiling. "He must have missed you, for I met him a minute ago. I suppose you are going to this new play there is on at the Cinema."

"Oh, I don't know," said Caroline vaguely. "I don't see much of Wilf now. Lovely night, isn't it?"

This was crude but sufficient, and the woman went on, leaving Caroline once more aimlessly pondering. At last she began to walk slowly down the Avenue to the Creddles' house, calling out at the door as usual: "Hello, aunt!"

Mrs. Creddle at once came out of the kitchen, her jolly face rather anxious. "You never came near yesterday, Carrie. We couldn't think what had gotten you."

"I was busy at home when I wasn't at the prom.," said Caroline. "I've come now to see if Winnie would like to go with me to the pictures."

"Well——" Mrs. Creddle hesitated. "Your uncle was in a fine taking on Thursday night. He seems to have an idea in his head that you were with somebody you daren't speak about. But you'd never have aught to do with a married man, I'm sure, Carrie."

"Well, you may make your mind easy, aunt. The man I was with was single. But I'm not going to say anything more about him. If I have to be answerable to you and uncle for every young fellow I chance to walk home from the prom. with——"

"You know we don't expect that," said Mrs. Creddle, still a little uneasy. "But I told your uncle I could trust you, and I do."

"Where is uncle?" said Caroline, seizing on the nearest pretext for changing the subject.

"Oh, he's gone to the Buffaloes," said Mrs. Creddle; and though her tone implied contempt and disapproval, it was but the natural prejudice of all good women for an institution purely masculine. "They have a Grand Council or some such rubbish to-night," she added; then she raised her voice and called "Winnie!" and imparted the joyful news to a little, rosy-faced girl whose eyes shone with ecstasy. To go to the pictures—at night— and with Cousin Carrie—Life could hold no more, and she sped off to change her frock, like an arrow from the bow.

Caroline had turned away and was staring rather moodily out of the window. Then she felt a hand on her arm. "Carrie, it wasn't young Mr. Wilson you were with, was it?" Mrs. Creddle said in a low voice.

In the involuntary start which followed the words she had her answer; letting her hand drop, she turned an agitated face towards Caroline. "Then you weren't after no good on Thursday night. Your uncle was right. Oh,

Carrie, how could you—with him going to be married in a fortnight? I should have thought you would have more self-respect."

Caroline swung round upon her, eyes ablaze. "Who told you I was with Mr. Wilson? You don't want to listen to everything you hear in Thorhaven, surely! And if I was, I was doing no wrong."

"I don't know how you could, Carrie," repeated Mrs. Creddle. "Trapesing about at night with Miss Laura's young man when you ought to have been abed—and after the way she has always treated us all. Why, the very frock Winnie is putting on now is made out of one of hers. I should take shame to try and make mischief between her and her young man, and with him going to be married directly."

"Don't talk such rot, aunt. I have done nothing to be ashamed of," said Caroline rudely, "and I've not set eyes on him since Thursday night. You may talk about Miss Laura—but I owe her nothing. I've paid all back, and more." She paused a moment, but pride, suspense, emotion unnaturally repressed—all combined to betray her into saying what she had never meant to say to any human being. "You think I've behaved badly, do you? Well! I might have taken him away from her altogether. He wanted to throw her over, only I wouldn't have it."

"Oh!" Mrs. Creddle gasped; then went on in a low tone of apprehension and unhappiness. "I didn't think it was as bad as that, Carrie."

"Bad!" Caroline stared with genuine surprise at this reception of her bomb-shell. "He wanted to *marry* me, I tell you."

Mrs. Creddle shook her head. "Poor Miss Laura! Well, I didn't think he was that sort, but you never know." She paused, then said gently: "My dear little lass, don't you know all men talk like that when they want to make fools of silly girls? I don't suppose there's hardly a girl gone wrong in Thorhaven but the man has sworn he wanted to marry her. It's a trick as common as sin."

"You don't know what you're talking about! You've lived among a low lot in this terrace until your mind has got poisoned," cried Caroline, maddened with anger and shame. "You're a wicked woman to have such horrible thoughts. I'm telling you the truth. May I die to-night if I aren't!"

"Oh, Carrie!" said Mrs. Creddle, wincing as if she had been struck. "How can you speak to me like that? I don't doubt you think it is all true. I don't doubt he said he would throw her over and marry you. But he didn't mean it. You never suppose he is going to give up Miss Laura and all that money, to marry a girl that is nobody and has nothing; I can't believe it! I never should believe it unless I saw you with his wedding-ring on your finger."

"You can believe or not, as you like," replied Caroline, regaining a little of her self-control. "At any rate, you must swear to keep it to yourself, or I will never tell you anything again as long as I live."

"I shan't want to spread such news abroad, you may be sure," said Mrs. Creddle. "But you must promise me not to trust yourself with him alone any more, Carrie. You don't know men as I do, and he can't be up to any good if he talks like that to you."

"Oh, very well," said Caroline, looking out of the window.

"I can see he's got hold of you," said Mrs. Creddle anxiously. "Oh dear! I don't know what I am to do. I daren't tell your uncle, for there's no saying what that would lead to. But you must be fond," she continued, exasperated, "if you think he really wants to make you his wife. Just fancy your marrying a relation of Miss Ethel's! Why, she'd fall down dead on the spot!"

"That wouldn't stop me," said Caroline grimly. "Lots of matches far more unequal than that come off nowadays. But you may make your mind easy. I aren't going to marry him—and I aren't going to behave in the way you seem to be afraid of, either. Only I'll just tell you this, aunt—I can never, never feel the same to you again after what you've said."

"Well, I can't help it!" answered Mrs. Creddle. "You'll come to thank me some day, Carrie, and I suppose I shall have to wait for that." All the same, the good woman's lip was trembling.

But Caroline, angry and dry-eyed, went to the door and called in a shrill voice: "Winnie! Winnie! Are you ready?"

Once outside, however, in the broad evening light, with the cool wind from the sea touching her face and the colours of the girls' bright dresses on the road growing faint, like flowers in a garden at sunset, Caroline began to feel somewhat less bitterly towards Mrs. Creddle. She remembered that her aunt had been in service as a girl, and that no self-respecting maid-servant of those days would have walked out late at night with a man who was a relative of their mistress, nor would any decent-living gentleman have suggested such a thing. But Aunt Creddle forgot that she was a business girl—self-poised, making her own position in the world as she chose.

Still her pride continued to smart even when she reached the little Thorhaven picture house. She sat down in the semi-darkness and fixed her eyes mechanically on the screen before her, but very little of Winnie's clear happiness communicated itself to her. After a while, however, she did begin to feel less miserable, because no one can be the cause of that rippling joy in a delighted child without being touched by it a little. But her main feeling was relief. At last she was free to be as utterly wretched as she liked. No one could peer into her mind as she sat there, apparently enjoying herself; she was wrapped in a secrecy so deep that no human being could touch even the fringe of what she was thinking about, for Winnie's remarks were only like the chirp of a bird on the window-sill when the window is closed.

But beneath all her restless unhappiness she was still certain that every word Godfrey said to her on Thursday night was sincere. A sort of nobleness in her own love—despite the flippant beginnings of it—made her able to believe that he had not considered money or ambition any more than she had done. It was the defenceless kindness of Laura herself which had conquered them both. They were unable deliberately to deal her such a blow.

But across her thoughts came the legend on the screen after the whirl of moving figures. At first she followed the words without being aware of them; when all at once they leapt into her consciousness with a sort of shock.

"I swear I want to marry you!"

Immediately on that a man appeared on the screen with a girl in his arms, but Caroline was not going to let her mind accept any possible relationship between this story and her own. Then Aunt Creddle's speech forced itself through the barrier she tried to put up and she had to remember: "Men always talk like that, Carrie. Don't you know that men always talk like that when they want to get over a girl?"

She moved restlessly in her seat, turning to Winnie: "This is a silly film."

But she had to go on thinking about it. Supposing Aunt Creddle were right? No, she couldn't be!

The memory of Godfrey's face as he looked up at her on the cliff ledge after she had refused him came back more vividly than the picture on the screen. That was real. If she were to doubt him, she must doubt the sea booming on the sands and the moon in the sky——

But if men did always say that? He might love her. She could not believe that he felt no real love for her then. But could he be wanting her love and everything else as well—like the man in the film?

She remembered that at the beginning of the interview he had suggested their being friends after his marriage. Could it be that he really had that in his mind all the time? Did he somehow know—though he loved her so then, and really meant what he said—that he was not going to mean it twenty-four hours later?

Suddenly she felt an overwhelming desire to ask him these questions. She must know. She must have an answer. It was all very well to say they would not meet again. When she said it she meant it most sincerely; but there must be some sort of settling up before they parted for the whole of their lives. It could not be cut off short like that; just a kiss and running away down a dark garden. They must for once know exactly where they stood before the shutter went up and they could never truly look into each other's thoughts any more.

She turned to the child, who sat wide-eyed and rosy-cheeked, staring at the pictures. "I say, Winnie, I think we must be going home now," she said. "It's getting late."

She spoke gently, with a guilty consciousness of dragging Winnie away from a rare treat; but her restlessness would not let her sit still watching these changing, grimacing faces any longer.

Poor Winnie looked a little crestfallen but cheered up under the promise of chocolates, and a minute or two later they were outside in the starlit night, tasting the salt freshness of the air.

Caroline halted a moment, looking down, taking no notice of Winnie, then she said abruptly:

"We'll go by Beech Lane."

"But that's so dark," pleaded Winnie, looking up anxiously, sensitive as children are to the changed atmosphere when something goes wrong in the mysterious grown-up world.

"Oh no; not with the houses still lit up," said Caroline.

"There's such a lot of trees. I hate them old trees," said Winnie under her breath.

But Caroline did not hear her, and the two walked on silently, side by side, under the shadow of the large beech trees which formed an avenue beside the pavement. They went so very slowly that Winnie asked if Caroline were tired, but receiving no answer she plodded on, still full of the vague puzzled discomfort which all children know, and which they never speak of to any human soul. At last she felt the hand in her own close nervously, and then two people emerged from a gateway in front of them.

"Oh!" she said, in her high little voice, "there's Mr. Wilson and Miss Temple. They're going into the house. I like Miss Temple, don't you? She gave mother——"

"Hush!" interrupted Caroline, her whole being absorbed in watching the couple who now stood together in the bright light which streamed from the open door.

"Coming in, Godfrey?" said Laura. Caroline could hear quite plainly from her dark ambush under the beeches.

Then followed a moment's silence, during which Caroline's heart beat so loudly that it almost seemed to her as if they must hear the thump! thump! thump! ever so far away, like a sound of drums beating. Then Godfrey said: "Oh yes; I'll come in. It is only about half-past nine."

She went first into the house, and he waited outside a moment with the light streaming through the doorway full on his face. All at once Caroline started to run—she must see him alone. She must speak to him.

"Cousin Carrie!" piped Winnie. "You're hurting my hand! You're hurting my hand!" But the door closed before they got across the road, and they were alone in the dark lane.

Caroline looked at that shut door, moved by an emotion which was not only the outcome of the experience of the moment, but which was also a part of her very flesh and blood. Her own mother. Aunt Creddle, Aunt Ellen, generations of women before them—all had lived "in service" and had watched the drama of life going on behind room doors which were always closed lest "the servants" should hear or see. And so acute had these senses become, sharpened by closed doors, that they always did see and hear, though they did not in the least resent this attitude of their employers, considering it just a part of the existing scheme of life.

But Caroline was different; and as she walked slowly along with Winnie disconsolately trudging by her side, she had an angry sense of being shut out from all sorts of things which she had as much right to possess as any other girl. She hated that shut door—Laura and Godfrey inside, and herself outside; then she thought how easily she could destroy all that if she liked, and how Laura's easy, flowery courtship was only possible because *she* allowed it.

Winnie spoke again and had to be answered; then Caroline went back to the aching round of thoughts again. She wouldn't be put aside like that— knowing nothing. She would give up, but she would not be left outside, guessing what was going on behind closed doors.

She tramped along, dull, dry-eyed, assailed by a strange feeling that she belonged nowhere, neither to Aunt Creddle's sort, nor to Laura's; yet all the time passionately aware that she was a "business girl" and as good as anybody.

Then there was Winnie again. Well, poor kid, she'd had no sort of an evening—— "Look here, Winnie, I'll take you again next week and we'll stop all the time."

"Honour bright?" said Winnie.

"Honour bright!" said Caroline. So Winnie cheered up, because she knew Cousin Carrie did not break promises.

Chapter XVI
New-Comers

During the night the wind freshened, then for three days it blew half a gale from the south-west. The sea was no longer a playfellow for little boys and girls, but a monster whose white fangs gleamed through the grey-blue water far out towards the horizon, ready to crunch the bones of ships and sailors alike with a sort of roistering glee.

A few visitors still fought their way up and down the promenade; and if of a sanguine temperament, they shouted above the wind, as they passed Caroline in the pay-box, that this really *ought* to blow the cobwebs away! But the furnished houses and apartments near the sea, where a turn-up bed on the landing could not be obtained for love or money six weeks ago, were now mostly empty. Even the visitors from Flodmouth who had remained in Thorhaven because they were so near home, began to think comfortably of lighted streets, theatres, cinemas, concerts—a general settling down to their ordinary routine of work and play.

When Caroline came out of the pay-box at the tea hour, she also realized that the season was over. A sort of flat finality lay over everything, despite the crispness of the air and the aromatic, clean fragrance of the masses of sea-weed which had been torn from the floor of the ocean in the storm and now lay drying on the shore.

Well, that was all over. She said so to herself as she walked away, feeling dull, resigned—it would be all the same a hundred years hence.

She had not seen Godfrey since that night on the way from the cinema when she and Winnie caught a glimpse of him from under the dark shadow of the trees, therefore it was plain that he must be avoiding her. He knew her hours at the promenade, and could easily have said a word in passing through even if he did not wish for anything more. He had taken her at her word; but being a woman, the desire to talk everything out grew during those three long stormy days to an agony of exasperation which was almost worse to bear at the moment than the loss of Godfrey himself.

After passing out of the promenade she came back again, saying to Lillie over her shoulder that she would go home by the cliff because she had a headache and a blow would do it good. She told herself the same thing. But beneath all that she was eagerly aware that Godfrey's lodgings lay in that direction. As she went down the terrace she could see the windows all open and the landlady moving about inside with a duster. For a moment she stood perfectly still, experiencing that sensation of physical sickness which comes from sudden emotional disappointment. She did not think at all, only suffered under the maddening frustration of her desire to have it all out with Godfrey once more before they finally parted. The waves and the sky did not exist for her, though they would always give dignity to the memory of what passed between Godfrey and herself that night on the cliff top. For while the seaside accords with frothy impermanence in love as no other background seems able to do, it is because those playing at passion feel subconsciously how little their light loves matter in face of that unchangeableness. Caroline stood there until she recovered herself; then the landlady came to shake the duster from the window and she walked slowly towards the Cottage.

The ladies were already seated at tea when Caroline opened the front door. Miss Ethel at once rose from the table with a dish of jam in her hand. "Caroline's tea," she said briefly.

"But you have not taken any yourself," objected Mrs. Bradford. "And I must say I don't see why Caroline should have it when our stock is getting so low."

"We promised to board and lodge her properly in return for her service, and I'm going to do it," said Miss Ethel with a tightening of the lips.

"Well, no one can say she has done her fair share of the bargain; at least, during the last few days," said Mrs. Bradford. "She seems in a sort of dream. Here! give me a bit more of that jam before you take it away."

"Caroline has never forgotten to bring my morning tea once since I was ill," said Miss Ethel. "But she certainly does not seem herself now. I don't know what is the matter with her."

"Got her head full of young men, no doubt," said Mrs. Bradford. "It makes some girls like that, of course."

She glanced instinctively at her husband's picture, speaking as one having first-hand information on all amatory matters.

Miss Ethel went into the kitchen where Caroline was already lifting the kettle from the fire; but when the girl turned round, her face looked so queer and drawn despite the colour which the wind had whipped into her cheeks, that Miss Ethel felt sorry. Still, the barrier of "the room door" had not been more immovably established in the consciousness of Aunt Ellen and Aunt Creddle, than the iron law of not "talking to the servants" in the minds of Miss Ethel and Mrs. Bradford. They had been so trained in the idea—though, it only became general about a hundred and fifty years ago—that when Miss Ethel now wanted to speak of Caroline's unhappy looks as one simple, ordinary human being to another she could not manage to do it. She meant to be kind and yet was obliged to assume the tone and manner—throwing her voice flute-like, as it were, across a gulf neither must cross—which her mother had always employed in speaking to the servants.

"Oh! Caroline," she said, placing the jam on the table. "I thought you might like some of this for your tea. It is very stormy out to-night, is it not? I hope you have not caught cold?"

She had a habit of beginning that way—"Oh! Caroline"—when she intended to give an order or make a request.

In making her perfunctory reply, Caroline never imagined for one moment that her own healthy appetite was often satisfied at Miss Ethel's expense. She had bargained for food, and food was there; and there was an end of it. But the front-door bell rang, and something in Miss Ethel's expression did then pierce her self-engrossment.

"Is anything the matter, Miss Ethel?"

"No, no." Miss Ethel stood there, pressing her thin hands together—striving to speak calmly. "It is only the people to look over the house, I expect." Then she turned round and walked with her head erect across the hall.

The door opened to disclose a short, thin, alert man with a taller, well-nourished woman in handsome clothes, wearing a thick coating of scented powder on her full cheeks and thick nose. Over her whole person was written in characters for all to read the consciousness of having plenty of money. It was new to her, and never for a moment could she forget it; while her husband also fed *his* satisfaction in having plenty of money every time he looked at her. And yet they were not unkindly people; ready to do a kindness if it did not take away from them any of the luxuries, pleasures, delightful enviousness in others less successful, which gradually would give them atrophy of the soul.

So they thought good-naturedly enough, that though the old girl looked a bit frosty and forbidding, that was no wonder—it must be a nasty jar to have to turn out of a house where you had lived so many years. And they made every allowance for the somewhat ceremonious manner in which she conducted them through the rooms.

"Ah yes; when I used to see you come into the front seats at the Flodmouth concerts with your respected father, and me in the shilling gallery, I little thought—— But it's one down and the other come up in these days, Miss Wilson. Same all the world over."

"Look, William!" said the wife, jogging her husband's arm. "That's a beautiful old bureau." Then she turned to Miss Ethel. "I dare say you have a lot of old furniture here that will be too big for your little house. Couldn't we offer to relieve you of some of it? I could do very well with that bureau and no doubt other things besides."

William whipped out his pocket-book. "Yes, Miss Wilson, you just say what you want to part with, and I'll have the lot valued by anybody you like. Pity to let the things go out of the house." He paused, suddenly noticing the grey shade on Miss Ethel's face: then added encouragingly: "You're quite in the fashion, you know, Miss Wilson. Everybody's doing it, from dukes downwards."

"Of course," said Miss Ellen. [Transcriber's note: Ethel?]

Mrs. Bradford sat stolidly silent, taking no part in the affair, not even when the little man said in a low voice: "Deaf, I see. A great affliction—a great affliction!"

At last they had seen everything, and stood once more in the hall before the open door. "Well, we came just as a matter of form," said the husband. "Never do to buy a pig in a poke, you know! But we shall go straight to Mr. Wilson and tell him we have decided to buy. You may make your mind at rest about that. Of course, there is a good deal to be done inside. But what I say is, it is a gentleman's house."

Then the wife said, glancing through the open door. "Oh! by the way, Miss Wilson, we wondered if you would mind our man coming in one day to dig up the privet hedge? You know labour is so difficult to get in Thorhaven, and we happen to have a man engaged for another month; so perhaps you——" Her voice trailed off into silence, for she was a little abashed by that look in Miss Ethel's pale eyes. "It won't look so pretty, of course, but it will let light and air into the house."

"Oh yes," said Miss Ethel, smiling with strained lips.

Then they went down the drive, leaving her there in the doorway staring at the privet hedge. Over the hedge, a fire had just been lighted in the scarcely completed bungalow, so that the white smoke streamed like a flag from the tall chimney, just moved a little from the south so that it swung over towards the Cottage. A week or two more and the hedge would be down. There would be no barrier at all between this quiet garden and all those rows of houses which had been marching on, nearer and nearer, ever since the first one was built. As Miss Ethel stood there, she felt beaten. She knew at last, what she had fought so hard not to know, that the powers against her in the world were too strong—that her opposition was ridiculous and futile. Nothing that she could ever say or do would make the slightest difference.

She returned to the room where Mrs. Bradford was sitting. "They will be sending some one to take up the hedge in a few days," she said.

"You don't mean it!" exclaimed Mrs. Bradford, startled into animation. "Oh, what a thing it is to be without a man in a matter like this! I know my dear husband would never have allowed it."

But Miss Ethel was at the window again, quietly looking out. "They say it will let light and air into the house. It won't look so pretty, but it will let light and air into the house."

Then they ceased speaking for the moment because Caroline had come into the room to take away the tea-tray; but before she had closed the door, Mrs. Bradford began again, still for her excitedly: "Ethel! Mrs. Graham ran in for a minute while you were upstairs, and she says Laura Temple's wedding is put off." There came a sudden crash of crockery just beyond the door. "Caroline!" cried Miss Ethel, "have you let the tray fall?"

Caroline did not answer at first; then she said in a low voice: "There's nothing broken, Miss Ethel."

But she did not move away—only forced her hands to hold the tray steadily so that they should not know she was there. The next moment she heard Miss Ethel cross the room and was obliged to go back to the kitchen.

There she stood washing up over the sink, seething with a conflict which almost maddened her. The old habit of Aunt Creddle and Aunt Ellen— grown into an instinct in course of generations—to guess, and listen for chance words, and piece together any drama that was going on "in the room" because their own lives were so circumscribed, fought with her own free impulse to return openly and ask the plain question: "Do you know why Miss Temple's engagement is broken off?"

The conflict made her feel terribly over-excited and nervous; but she had one over-mastering reason for not obeying that impulse to ask a direct question—she was afraid lest these two women might see she was in love with Godfrey. Then she happened to glance at the clock, and saw she was already late for the promenade; but as she hurried down the drive she heard the whistle of a railway engine and stood perfectly still just as if some one had called to her. But that was the five-twenty-five train, of course. That by which Godfrey invariably returned when he had spent the day in the city, was half an hour later. If she waited outside the station until it came in, she would be certain to see him. He *must* speak to her then. This maddening agony of uncertainty and suspense would be over at least.

But as she hurried along to the station with the moist west wind in her face, she saw—behind those engrossing thoughts—the other girl waiting angrily to be released from the pay-box. Still, that didn't matter to Caroline. Nothing mattered in the world, but getting that talk with Godfrey. For she had reached a point now, when all these business men and shopping ladies who began to flow past her from the platform—drawing their scarves closer, and buttoning their coats as they merged into the cool, salt air after the warmer atmosphere of the city—seemed no more to her than flies buzzing round a path she was bent on following.

Wilf came past, taking long strides and wearing a new hat which he removed slightly; giving a sideways, condescending nod which said as plainly as words: "If you're waiting for *me*, miss, it's no go!"

But though she nodded in return, she was not actually aware of him. Her heart beat unevenly and she felt a suspense which ran through every nerve and every vein—she had no feeling beyond it. Her face was ashen as she stood by the entrance to the station, with the breakers beyond looking cruel in the cold light. Her eyes shone black, owing to the pupils being so distended, but she appeared pinched and quiet as she stood there, at the edge of the crowd, for her whirling emotions had now reached that point which looks like stillness.

All of a sudden the blood rushed up over her forehead, and she instinctively put her hand to her heart because it seemed to be leaping out of its place. Here was Godfrey at last, walking with another man. She moved forward and stood directly in his way, so that he must see her. "Good evening," he said, then continued his conversation with the broad, prosperous-looking merchant who walked by his side.

Caroline remained planted there, staring after them with an almost foolish expression on her face. She could not take it in. It seemed incredible. Then the two men vanished round the corner, and at the same moment she heard a girl saying in her ear: "Cheer up, Carrie! If Wilf hasn't caught this, he will get the next. He isn't dead."

"What do you mean?" said Carrie, but her voice sounded muffled and vague, even to herself.

"Why, you came to meet your boy, didn't you? And he hasn't turned up. That's what you looked like, anyway," said the girl, laughing.

Carrie made an immense effort to fight off that feeling of faintness, saying jerkily: "Oh, well, I'm off with Wilf, you know." But the words seemed to echo in some great, vague place a long distance away.

Chapter XVII
The Benefit Concert

During the evening and many hours of the night Caroline remained in a white heat of anger and hurt pride which left no room for regret. It was true, then, that Godfrey had only been behaving to her all the time as Aunt Creddle said gentlemen did behave to working girls upon whom they bestowed their attentions. She'd been treated exactly like any little ignorant servant girl waiting at a street corner for her young man: just such a one as her aunts and her mother had been; and yet she felt violently that she was different. In the middle of the night she woke to find herself muttering: "I aren't going to stand it! I aren't going to stand it!" Then she bit the sheet to prevent herself from breaking out into a storm of weeping. She loved him so, but was no longer certain of his love. She could give him up almost gladly if he loved her and would always love her—but this was more than she could bear. There seemed to her no paradox in that—it was just what she felt.

Then she saw his heavily cut face on the darkness, as he had looked when he walked past her with that other man—both of them solid, self-contained, out of her reach! And with that the cold wave of anger swept over her again, overwhelming her. "I can't stand it! I aren't going to stand it. He'd no right to treat me like that, as if I were dirt beneath his feet. I'm as good as he is."

So the conflicting thoughts went on during the night hours; all the doubts and feelings which she had inherited, or had imbibed from the Creddles, warring with her own independence and pride. A girl like herself was good enough for any man. He'd no right to insult her by passing her like that in the street when they'd kissed as they did on the cliff top. She'd given him up, but she was going to be treated properly—not like a girl who had done something of which they were both ashamed. And again the helpless threat: "I aren't going to stand it!"

At last it was time to get up, and after a while to go down to the promenade. She was by now so exhausted with emotion that she could not feel any more and let her perceptions drift vaguely over outside things. A bill was up on the road-side, announcing the Benefit Concert for the band for that evening; another advertised second-hand tents and folding chairs for sale, cheap. A girl told her about a tent that had blown down the day of the gale, revealing a fat lady in a bathing towel—behaviour of rude Boreas which seemed to have put an end to bathing from tents for the season.

Then a man came down the road with a barrow, crying, "Meller pears! Fine meller pe-a-a-rs!" Caroline bought some to take to Aunt Creddle, though she had had no definite thought of going there when she started ten minutes earlier than usual, but the ache of her exhausted emotion drew her subconsciously towards the jolly, serene nature as a hurt child runs to its mother.

The house door was open, so she walked straight in and put the pears down on the table. But she did not kiss her aunt, because she instinctively feared that the slightest breath of emotion might upset her self-control. "I bought these off a barrow. Don't know if they'll be sweet," she said. "Can't stop!"

"Sit down a minute," said Mrs. Creddle. "You look fit to drop. Aren't you feeling well, Carrie?"

"Oh, I'm all right," she answered impatiently. "What's that you are ironing?"

"It's some curtains for Miss Temple. I was there ironing yesterday, but didn't get these finished."

Caroline sharply turned with her back to the kitchen, looking out of the window. "Did they say anything about the wedding being put off?"

"Yes. Miss Laura's got a chill. Something to do with her digestion. She can't scarcely eat nothing."

"Oh!" Caroline could not say another word.

"Of course, it's hard on Mr. Wilson; but I think she's in the right on it. No use going away to them grand hotels if you can't enjoy the food," pursued Mrs. Creddle.

"Did you—did you hear how long it was put for?" said Caroline.

"Not exactly, as you may say," answered Mrs. Creddle. "Miss Panton came into the kitchen while I was there, and she said delays was dangerous. You know her way. She seemed to think it would be next month." She paused, then added uncomfortably: "I was on pins and needles for fear they might have heard about you and Mr. Wilson, Carrie, you know—being about the lanes at night together, and that. But I'm sure they hadn't." She paused again. "Well, I aren't sorry you had a lesson that night you were locked out, Carrie. Your mother and I had the same sort of temptations when we were out in placing—though you mayn't think it. There was a young gentleman from college in my last situation who begged me almost on his bended knees to walk out with him, but I knew what that led to."

She paused again. "Cheer up, lass; it hurts a bit at the time, but it's all for the best. Once bitten, twice shy."

"You're always talking about what people did when *you* were young," said Caroline, turning away abruptly.

"I know that. Things is very altered since my day," said Mrs. Creddle. "But there's some things——"

"I've no patience with people like you, aunt," said Caroline. "You know everything has changed, and yet you go on expecting girls to be the one thing that hasn't. It isn't common sense."

She was flinging out of the kitchen, when Mrs. Creddle caught her up and put a motherly arm about her. "Good-bye, my lass. You think nobody's felt like you before about a young man, but they have."

"I don't know what you're talking about. I've a bit of a head, but that's all," said Carrie.

After that she went away. But all the same she was a little comforted—real, disinterested love being the one ointment that can soothe tender hearts not yet cauterized by pain.

So the day passed; then the next wore on towards evening, with no sign of Godfrey. And all through the long hours, Caroline sat in the pay-box looking out of her little window—small, set face, very pale, and bright eyes intently watching—like some creature of the wild behind a gap in the thick leafage.

Now it was past sunset. The residents of Thorhaven had taken possession of their town again and the few visitors who remained were sprinkled about inconspicuously among the audience in the concert hall—the dominant factor no longer. Caroline exchanged greetings with many of her acquaintances who emerged from the seclusion entailed by letting rooms or vacating houses, and now shook their feathers like hens coming off the nest with the pleasant knowledge of a nest-egg successfully achieved. "Pretty good season, considering," ran the verdict; but the general mind was a happy one, in spite of a certain feeling of exhaustion. "Pickles!" said Lillie's mother. "I give you my word, Carrie, one lot ate cheese and pickles after the promenade every night to that degree it fair curdles my inside to think of. But as I say, each person's inside is their own. Live and let live, say I." And the good woman hurried on to spend part of the proceeds of this wise neutrality, her Sunday hat still quite like new from lack of use, and a holiday spirit radiating from her rather worn features.

Caroline had responded to all these greetings, but she was glad when the concert began in the promenade hall and only a few stragglers passed through the barrier at long intervals. Once more she was free to resume that silent, intent watch which had occupied nearly the whole day.

But night was coming on fast now—with a heavy ground-swell and a wild streak of orange on the western sky. Caroline never thought once of the sea, and certainly was not conscious of being affected by it—she was, in fact, not aware of it at all. Yet it was just because she did most deeply respond to it that her affair with Godfrey was lifted for her beyond the trivial into those regions where passion really has dignity. That interview of theirs on the cliff top would have been poignant for both if it had taken place in a dingy back sitting-room; but something must have been absent— that unforgettable thrill which comes when beauty is joined to great emotion.

After a while, Caroline saw a woman leave the concert hall to cross the promenade, which already gleamed darkly with rain-drops. As she went through the turnstile she said: "I doubt we shall have a wet night." Then followed a storm of applause from the hall. "There!" added the woman, "I wish I could have stopped for the encore, but I had to get away, though I was forced to squeeze past Miss Temple and her gentleman on my way out. She does look bad, my word! Them that said it was all a tale about her being ill, have only to look at her. Well, good night."

Caroline waited a moment, then thrust her head forward and peered round the black space between her and the hall; and as she did so, her likeness to some watching wild creature became intensified. Then she withdrew her head, rose from her seat and came out of the pay-box, looking over her shoulder. With light, quick steps she went round the glass walls of the hall until she reached a place through which she could see the occupants of the front seats. Just as she came to a stand, seeking for Laura with heart throbbing and every pulse alert, the singer returned to give the encore.

The voice was long past its prime, but a window above had been opened wide for ventilation and the song could be heard clearly enough. As Caroline peered in vain through the glass dimmed by heat and human breath, the sentimental words floated out over her head; and the heavy organ-like accompaniment of the ground-swell made them more than ever ephemeral. A few bars of music, sounding so thin and strange against the booming of the sea, and then the next verse:

Now we are young,
Life's meaning all grows clear,
Does he but whisper low:
"My dear—my dear!"

She pressed her forehead close to the glass, trying to keep back the tears, for she despised crying. Then the singer began again—the clear articulation almost all she had left:

And if we part,
I shall not cease to hear
For ever in my heart:
"My dear—my dear!"

Caroline could not keep the tears back any longer. They would come, and she wiped them away with her fingers as she walked away. But the singer was evidently roused by applause to an extra effort, for the voice gained for the moment some of the timbre of her triumphant youth, and Caroline could hear more and more softly as she went farther off:

When we are old
Some love-words disappear,
But this goes all the way;
"My dear—my dear!"

She did not see the sentimentality of the song because she liked it, just as she liked the simple love-stories with bright covers; and she had hardly time to dry her eyes before the band began to play God Save the King, and the people to surge through the large gates which were now set open. As soon as she could shut up the pay-box she slipped away into the darkness of the promenade, to escape the crowd who went mostly by the high road. A few steps beyond the north exit took her into absolute solitude, but the rain which was already falling quickly made her afraid of venturing far along the slippery path. The sea and sky were all dark—no white breakers on the heavy swell and no stars in the sky. She felt unutterably sad and deserted, standing there for a moment before she turned up the little terrace which led to the main road. But though she told herself that she was going this way because she had been crying and wished to meet no one, she knew, behind that, that she was lying to herself. She *had* to know why she really came this way, and what she meant to do, because she had an honest soul.

Then she turned round and went up the uneven road between the dark little houses in the terrace. Only one house still remained lighted downstairs, though the upper blinds were nearly all illuminated from within. Caroline's eyes were fixed on that one house as she went along, and without allowing herself time to think she opened the little iron gate. Then she paused a moment, glancing up towards the attic bedroom where the woman with whom Godfrey lodged was already taking off her tightly curled fringe, and the uncompromising corsets in which she barricaded herself during the waking hours.

With a long knowledge of Thorhaven ways Caroline gently turned the front-door handle, and was not surprised to find the door left on the latch against Godfrey's return. She entered very quietly, tip-toeing down the passage, and went straight into the front room where stood lamp, kettle and other preparations for a light meal.

Caroline breathed hard as she reached the middle of the room, experiencing the odd sense of having been followed by unknown dangers which children know when they run down a long stairway in the dark. But here she was safe. The lamp—the chair—newspaper—the little meal set ready—all reassured her. Yet she was still standing, peering bright-eyed here and there, when a quick step sounded outside, and the next minute Godfrey hurried into the room. "You, here!" he said, staring at her, greatly startled. "What's the matter?"

"Nothing." She moved back towards the fireplace.... He had not kissed her; he had not even held out his hand. "I aren't going to stop," she said in a low tone. "I only wanted to know if—if your wedding was really broken off for the reason they said. I felt as if I must know. I—I thought perhaps she'd heard something about you and me."

"How should she hear anything?" he said. "The poor girl is ill enough, as anybody can see. But she would come to this rotten concert to-night in spite of all Miss Panton and I could say. She seems unable to keep quiet." He paused and added jerkily: "I suppose you know we were to have been married to-day?"

"Yes." Caroline felt the room swim round her, but she clutched the mantelpiece and kept quiet.

"I came for a couple of umbrellas. She and Miss Panton are waiting under shelter in the hall. I can't stay." He spoke abruptly, uneasily.

"Oh, I won't keep you." She moved a step or two forward and swayed a little, so that he was obliged to catch hold of her by the arm. The next second he was clasping her close while they looked into each other's eyes with a burning curiosity that must at all costs be satisfied. "Do you love me still? Do you love me still?" And yet there was absolute silence in the room while the question was asked and answered.

"Oh, I don't mind now," sobbed Caroline. "I don't mind now. It was only when I thought——"

"Hush!" said Godfrey, moving away. "What's that?"

"It sounds like Miss Armitage coming down," said Caroline, hurrying towards the door. "I'll slip out as quickly as I——" She drew back. "Oh!" Then pulled herself together as the landlady in curled fringe and long grey ulster entered the room, primming long, thin lips.

"Oh! Good evening, Miss Raby," said the woman. "I'm sorry if I intrude. I heard voices down below and I didn't know who it might be. I wasn't aware, Mr. Wilson, you had visitors."

"No more have I," said Godfrey lightly. "Miss Raby has just come with a message from Miss Wilson. I suppose you can't lend her an umbrella, Miss Armitage? I have to hurry away to the promenade with both mine. Miss Temple and Miss Panton are waiting for me there." He turned to Caroline. "I'm afraid I must hurry away. Good night."

As he went off. Miss Armitage said somewhat grudgingly: "If you wait a minute, I dare say I can find you an old umbrella some visitors left here in the summer."

"Please don't bother. I'm neither sugar nor salt," said Caroline pleasantly. "Good night, Miss Armitage."

And her happy tone was not all put on; because though the tangle and bitterness would come back again before the morning, she could realize nothing in the world now but the triumphant answer to that question she had wanted to ask during all those hours when she looked at the waves without seeing them and heard their moaning only inside her heart.

Chapter XVIII
Uprooting

Mrs. Bradford and Miss Ethel came out of the Cottage and walked through the garden in which—on so many windy, sunshiny mornings— they had done a little weeding or planting before they went to shop in the long street, where everybody knew them and everybody treated them with respect. "Yes, Miss Wilson. I'll be sure to let you have the middle cut, ma'am. Beautiful day for the time of year." But now there was a "Take it or leave it" attitude which grated very much on Miss Ethel's susceptibilities as she gave her small orders, and she felt thankful there was no shopping to be done on this particular morning. All the same, the errand on which she actually was bent made the way as painful to her as if she had been treading on sharp stones.

"I think Godfrey might have gone over the house with us, as he promised, instead of just leaving the key," she said.

"Did Caroline take the key in? I suppose there was no message?" said Mrs. Bradford.

"No: she said not. I asked her." Miss Ethel paused. "I thought there was something rather funny in her manner."

"What! You don't think there is anything in what the Grahams said?" exclaimed Mrs. Bradford, speaking far more alertly than usual.

"Of course I don't," said Miss Ethel.

"But Mr. Graham is sure he saw Godfrey go up to Caroline at the Gala on the promenade the minute our backs were turned. It was when he went back to buy those air-balloons for the children at the Home and he happened to look round."

"Well, what is there in that? I don't say he is by any means my ideal of a young man," said Miss Ethel. Then she added after a pause: "You must not dream of mentioning the subject to Caroline. It is not our affair."

They walked a few paces in silence, aware that they could not afford to send Caroline away even if she were a bad girl, and yet shamed within themselves by the knowledge.

"The Grahams seemed to think Godfrey has had serious money losses," remarked Mrs. Bradford at last. "Lucky he had Laura's money to fall back on."

"Well, I think she is lucky in having him to make the most of her capital," said Miss Ethel. "He has a wonderful head for business. Any difficulties that he may have will be only temporary." They were both talking without heeding particularly what they said, nervously engrossed by the errand on which they were bent.

But at last they turned the corner of Emerald Avenue, and the blank fact had to be faced. "That is our house, then. Number fifteen," said Miss Ethel.

So they went through the little iron gate, and an old man came hobbling across the street to speak to them. "Good morning, ladies," he said in a high trembling voice. "I hear you're going to live here. I hear my darter's a-going to have you for a neighbour. Well! well! Who'd a-thought it?"

His intention was kindly, but his manner showed a sort of triumph underneath: it was in some way gratifying to him that Miss Ethel, who used to give him tobacco and other little comforts, had come down to the same level as his daughter. Not that he had received anything lately, because Miss Ethel had nothing to give, while his son-in-law made good wages and his daughter let rooms. At any rate Miss Ethel missed the power to give far more than he missed the tobacco; and that from no desire to patronize—though perhaps she did like the gratifying glow of that feeling a little—but because of the real goodness and generosity at the bottom of her nature.

"I'm sure we shall be glad to have such good neighbours," she said pleasantly.

"Yes, yes. My darter's family wants for nothing. They've gotten one of these 'ere gramophones an all," chuckled the old man. "You'll hear it through the wall and it'll mebbe cheer you up if you feel dowly. But it's hard moving at your time of life."

Then he went off, chuckling and muttering to himself, and Mrs. Bradford and Miss Ethel walked up the tiny path to the house which was to be their home for the rest of their lives. But before they reached the door it opened from within, and there stood Laura Temple. She was smiling, and yet her kind eyes were bright with tears which she could scarcely keep from falling—for the two ageing women looked somehow so forlorn in the bright sunshine on the threshold of all this strangeness. But after the briefest pause Miss Ethel relieved the situation by saying briskly: "So you have opened the windows. Now that was good of you."

"Oh, Nanty did that. She's here, too," said Laura. Then they all went through the narrow passage into the front room.

"There is only one corner where I can have my chair," said Mrs. Bradford immediately. "Laura dear, those who lead an active life can't understand how important it is for anyone like me to have a chair in the right place. But you have not been well yourself. I can quite understand your not wanting to go away on a honeymoon when you are not feeling well. I shall never forget having a bilious attack on my own honeymoon. I would always recommend a small medicine chest as part of the wedding outfit—sore-throat remedies and gregory powder, and so on. My dear husband said that, so far as he was concerned, biliousness did not destroy romance; but there are bridegrooms and bridegrooms, and you never know until——"

"We'd better begin measuring the floor," interposed Miss Ethel uneasily, anxious to cut short this unusual loquacity on the part of Mrs. Bradford, which she knew to be caused by the general upset of looking forward to an entire change of place and routine. "Don't you think the old dining-room carpet will do very well here?"

She opened the room door suddenly to discover Miss Panton just outside suppressing her emotion with a handkerchief pressed to her lips. Now she was obliged to let it finally escape in a sort of whoop. "Oh! Excuse me. I can't help it! It's the thought of you here," she said excitedly. "I know silence is golden, but there are tibes—— And to see Miss Ethel going round on her hands and dees with a tape beasure as if it was only an ordinary spring cleaning——" Never had the catarrh been so marked and so marked in its effects on her m's and n's.

"Nonsense! We shall be quite comfortable here and much less work to do. Thousands of richer people than ourselves are having to move into smaller houses," said Miss Ethel; but she was touched all the same.

"I'm not sure my chair will stand in that corner," said Mrs. Bradford, going back to her great preoccupation. "I must measure it. I do wish I had it here."

"I can easily run and get the measurements," said Laura.

"You're sure it won't upset you," said Miss Panton. "You know you ought to take care."

"Of course not," said Laura. "I'm nearly all right again."

But she stood facing the strong light which fell through the uncurtained window, and her face looked very pale beneath the tan; it had the queer bleached appearance which is observable in such complexions even while the healthy brown and red still remain. There were dark marks underneath her eyes, too, which accentuated the faint lines near the mouth. Miss Ethel, glancing across at her was struck for the first time by the fact that Laura was not a young girl any more, though the effect of girlishness produced by her figure and the poise of her head still remained.

Then she went away to measure the chair, while Miss Ethel wrote some figures in a little book and remarked that she would now go up to the front bedroom.

"Then I'll just stay where I am," said Mrs. Bradford. "There is nothing for two to do, is there? And you know my legs, of course——" She did not trouble to be more explicit, because her unusual garrulity was dying down now Miss Panton and Laura had gone, and she knew Ethel would be reasonable enough to understand that the legs of a married lady could not be expected to go up and down stairs as easily as those of a spinster.

Miss Ethel herself so belonged to the generation when a married woman was necessarily on a different and higher level than an "old maid," that though she knew her sister in many ways to be a fool, she yet bowed to the unassailable superiority of the widow. She really did feel that the useless legs of her widowed sister were more worthy of consideration than her own unwedded limbs as she trudged upstairs.

When she spread the measuring tape across the floor in front of the window, her glance wandered for a moment to the house opposite where a fat woman in an untidy blouse was standing in the doorway laughing and talking with the milkman. A small child dragged a noisy cart along the pavement, eating at the same time a large piece of Yorkshire pie. Then a second woman opened the next door and joined the fun. They were all jolly together, self-satisfied. They had done well, and were relaxing after the rush of the season; but they seemed very far away from Miss Ethel as she looked out of the window.

Still she never thought of envying them their jollity and self-satisfaction. Deep in her heart she knew she would rather be herself with nothing, than such as they with everything. She had only a vague sense of uneasiness, which was deepened by the sound of the gramophone next door grinding out "Home, sweet Home." For her sake the old man—who lived with his daughter during the winter when lodgers were few—had sinned against the law which prohibited his use of the new gramophone. This was partly because he really wanted to cheer Miss Ethel, and partly because he realized his daughter's good fortune better when he thought of the ladies listening to him through the wall.

But Miss Ethel's attention was soon distracted, for a baby wailed in the house on the other side, and a fish cart went past ringing a loud bell to warn the women to run out with their dishes. The bell was harsh in tone, filling the street with clamour, and when the cart started again after a purchase the bell pealed afresh each time. It was some time before the desire of Emerald Avenue for the harvest of the sea was satisfied, but in the comparative silence which at last ensued, Miss Ethel pressed her hand to her forehead as she rose dizzily from her knees. For a moment or two the house opposite looked blurred, then the haziness passed off, and she saw the road lying empty in the grey light—the lace-curtained windows, the sideboard with a mirror back on the far side of the room, even the vase of faded flowers.

But despite the minute definiteness of it all, she had a most queer feeling of unreality. She told herself that this would probably be her home until she died, and that there was nothing to complain of—she ought to be ashamed to complain. But the words which were forming on the surface of her thoughts seemed to have no relation whatever to anything going on underneath. She could not, or would not try to see deep down, because that odd sense of unreality rather frightened her; but something rose up like an emanation—a presentiment, she would have called it, had she allowed herself to do so. But the whole idea of her living here seemed so pervaded with bleak unreality, as she stood there looking out of the window, that it seemed to be wiped out of the scheme of actual human happenings. Then from that under-swirl of feeling rose one definite thought: "I shall never live here."

She turned abruptly from the window, bracing herself by saying aloud: "Bless me! I'm getting like the old women in Back Hoggate. I shall soon be counting my ailing relatives over if a spark flies out of the candle." But even this comparison of herself with the superstitious inhabitants of the oldest part of Thorhaven did not drive away that unpleasant feeling, and she felt relieved by the sound of a human voice calling up the stairs: "Miss Ethel! I've brought the key. And I have put your lunch ready, and left the kettle on. I thought you might be glad of a cup of tea."

The voice, fresh, confident, full of abounding vitality, dispelled those queer sensations of Miss Ethel's. She came to the top of the stairs and thanked Caroline, for she had learned that she could no longer take good and willing service for granted. The extent, indeed, to which she had been bowed by circumstances, showed in her anxious, almost humble manner, as she hastened to add—despite her annoyance about the gossip concerning Caroline and Godfrey: "I hope you found the small beef-steak pie I left for your dinner? I forgot to tell you it was in the safe."

"Oh, I got all I wanted, thank you," said Caroline, adding as she went again down the passage: "I'll come straight in, Miss Ethel."

For she had felt very sorry for these two women as she busied herself about the house all the morning, doing her best to make things cheerful against their return. But on the way here, a few minutes ago, she had met Laura Temple on the road, and that put everything else out of her mind. She actually held her breath as they approached, wondering what would happen. If Laura had heard any of the gossip that was about the town her salutation—supposing she gave one at all—would be different.

But her pleasant "Good morning, Miss Raby," was just the same as usual; and though there might be a stiffness about Miss Panton's greeting, that lady never had been cordial.

But the brief encounter had left Caroline disturbed, confused, breathless—as if she had been running too fast for her strength. Her knees shook under her as she went on her way towards Emerald Avenue, though she looked just as usual—able to exchange a chaffing word with a boy of her acquaintance. For she, no less than other human beings, would be obliged to go through the tremendous crises of her emotional existence in the street, or at a party, or in a tram-car—her real self kept close, enshrouded by that strange cloak which hides every man from his neighbour.

Still it was obvious that Laura knew nothing. The marriage really had been put off for the reason stated. No one could doubt that who saw Laura's face even casually in the street.

Caroline had nearly reached Emerald Avenue when it occurred to her that Laura was probably going to the Cottage and would need her key. But she could not run after her with it. She felt a physical revulsion at the bare thought of speaking to a girl who was engaged to Godfrey—talking to him—receiving his kisses——

It had seemed almost easy, that first night on the cliff top, to behave decently about it all. But then everything had turned different. She could scarcely realize now how it had then seemed so clear, so entirely possible at once to give him up, and to be always certain of his love. The difficulties and confusions all came afterwards.

She told herself once more as she walked along that Godfrey could not possibly be such a cad as to throw over a poor girl who was crazy about him just before the wedding day, nor could he be meeting another girl on the sly at the same time.

And yet the sick trembling brought on by the sight of Laura remained until she reached Emerald Avenue. She had no room in her thoughts for the sorrows of others when she arrived with the key.

Miss Ethel came down directly she left, having finished measuring the floors; and after a while Laura came back to say that she had stupidly forgotten when she met Caroline on the way to ask her if the house were locked, so that she and Miss Panton could not get in, of course. She thought it strange that Caroline had not mentioned the key, as she had it in her hand; and after wondering about this a little they all went away, walking together to the end of the street. Here the ladies from the Cottage turned off towards the north, and when they had gone a little way in silence, Miss Ethel said: "Flamborough looks very clear to-day. We shall have rain." For she hoped by starting this subject to turn her sister's slow-moving thoughts away from the new house. She felt just then that she simply could not endure to discuss it.

But Mrs. Bradford did not want to talk about Flamborough.

"I do wish," she said, "Laura had got the measurements of my chair. I am afraid there may not be room for it on that side of the fire——" So all the way home, at intervals, she kept bemoaning the possible lack of space for her chair.

Miss Ethel felt very tired. But at last they reached the gate of the Cottage, and as they walked up the drive they saw that a man was at work taking up the privet hedge. He was doing it badly, mauling the fine roots in a way that made Mrs. Bradford for once almost energetic in her annoyance.

"Don't look! I can't bear to look at our poor hedge," she said, turning her head away.

Miss Ethel's glance rested indifferently on the man and the partially destroyed hedge. "What does it matter?" she said, and walked on to the front door.

"You mean, because we shall not be here?" said Mrs. Bradford uneasily, for even she felt there was something a little uncomfortable in her sister's voice and look.

But Miss Ethel's glance passed over the neat little lozenge-shaped leaves which lay torn from their place but still clinging to the branches, almost with indifference: then she went straight into the hall, making no reply, and Mrs. Bradford followed slowly, filled with the dull discomfort of the cat turned out of its basket. Her feeling was different from Miss Ethel's—less acute—but she was not in the least consoled by her vague knowledge that she was sharing this experience with thousands of middle-aged men and women all over Europe.

Chapter XIX
A Windy Morning

It was the last week of the Thorhaven season, and a gale from the south-west tore across the little town, blowing away all the remaining visitors—excepting a few barnacles who had moved into the cheap rooms or furnished houses, and intended to stay for the winter.

Miss Ethel heard the familiar sounds of windows rattling and chimneys roaring as they do in an old house, but she was so used to them that she never heeded; they formed part of the background of her life without which, she vaguely apprehended, she would appear as baldly incomplete as a figure cut out with sharp scissors from an old print.

But as she stood there on the landing she became gradually aware of another noise with which she was not familiar, for the simple reason that Ellen had never set the maid's door and window sufficiently wide open in a high wind to produce a gale rushing through the house with such a flap and clatter of blinds and curtains.

Miss Ethel frowned as she marched into the room for she saw the casement window set wide, banging to and fro on the metal fastener. A little more, and it would be blown clear out, to lie shattered on the path below. But when she had closed it, she was suddenly struck by the entire absence of that peculiar close odour which had always been present when the room was occupied by the immaculate Ellen and her predecessors. Now there was only the fresh feeling of salt air, mingled with a very faint fragrance of violets which came either from the soap or from the powder on the toilet table. A nail-polisher lay on the looking-glass, hastily thrown down; and that also witnessed to that bodily self-respect which Caroline shared with nearly all those other girls in Thorhaven who would have been in domestic service ten years ago, but now went daily to shops and offices. They meant to be the equal of any girls in the world, and they began by being personally "nice" in those secret ways, which are only apparent in the general effect. You could meet them anywhere up and down—clear skins sometimes too heavily powdered—bright hair—pink fingers with delicately tended finger-nails.

Caroline had gone off hurriedly that morning, because she wanted to do as much housework as she could before leaving for the promenade. She was sorry for Miss Ethel, who did not look at all well, though this feeling was blunted by her pre-occupation with her own troubles—for it had become quite plain that Godfrey was deliberately avoiding her.

At this moment she was walking quickly along the road, head to the wind; then, turning, found herself sheltered from west and south to some extent by the houses opposite the promenade. But once in the little pay-box she had to listen all day while the little window rattled unceasingly, and the boards creaked as the gale swept across them.

The weather remained like that during the whole week, and Caroline was on duty all day excepting for her meal-times. Occasionally a gleam of sun touched the white crests of the breakers, but immediately afterwards a sharp spatter of rain would drive in the faces of the few who were tempted out.

The hours seemed endless to Caroline as she sat there—listening to the howl and rattle of the wind, and the roaring of the sea, without knowing that she listened to them. But very gradually she began to feel in her spirit the effect of that deep, endless booming, and of the tremendous procession of the breakers that came on and on all day long. It made her almost dizzy, but when she turned for relief to the land, the promenade and the little town itself seemed only like leaves swept together by chance for a moment on the edge of a torrent. A horrid sense of the shortness of life assailed Caroline now, as it will sometimes assail young people when they are dispirited. She felt that cold breath from the immense spaces of eternity to which the young are still sensitive.

But the week would soon be over—— She consoled herself by that thought as she sat before the little window knitting a woollen coat to wear when she went to office in Flodmouth. Every now and then she glanced drearily at the grey waves with the white crests, coming on and on—— It was a rotten world, and she didn't care. What was the good of it all, anyway?

Then a subscriber passed through to the promenade; but her reply to his remark about the weather was as mechanical as her release of the iron turnstile. Directly he was gone she looked out to sea again, thinking now of a girl who had been drowned farther along the coast not long before. Well, she only wished the waves would come over the promenade and take her with them, then she'd be out of it all.

But she did not mean that really; because certain qualities she inherited from her sturdy Yorkshire ancestors would always prevent her from choosing the way of the neurotic. She would be brave enough to live out her life, though she had ceased to expect happiness as a right.

A sharp gust of rain on the window made her look down the promenade. Now the stray figures would come scurrying through again to their homes or lodgings, and she automatically prepared to release the turnstile quickly to oblige people in haste. Then, with a little leap of the pulses, she saw Aunt Creddle. It was Aunt Creddle, out at half-past eleven on baking-day, with her print, working dress ballooning under that old coat and the hair straggling over her face. Caroline jumped up and ran out of the pay-box, her knitting still in her hand, the shower of cold, sharp drops driving across her.

"What's the matter?" she cried. "Has one of the children got hurt?"

Mrs. Creddle so panted for breath that she could only sign with a toil-scarred hand for Caroline to go back into shelter, but on reaching a little protection from the wind she managed to gasp out:

"Nobody's ill. There's nothing the matter. Not in a manner of speaking. Can I come inside there?"

Caroline took her arm and put her into the chair, then shut the door in the side of the little wooden turret. They two seemed very close together in the midst of the storm and wind.

"Why, whatever made you come out like this?" said Caroline, removing the wet cloak. "You must have wanted a job, aunt."

Mrs. Creddle shook her head, her hand on her heart—for she was a stout woman and upset by her tussle with the elements. "You may be sure that it was something that wouldn't keep," she said at last. Then she burst forth: "Carrie, your uncle has been to Mr. Wilson! He's been and told him that if he ever catches you together again he'll break a stick over his back. He lost a couple of hours this morning, and he went and told him. Now he's gone to his work, and I come on here."

"What!" gasped Caroline, her eyes black in a face as white as death. "Uncle's dared to insult me by doing a thing like that? What made him do it?"

"He was at the Buffaloes last night, and when they came away he heard one man say to another that you was Wilson's fancy lady——" She paused and added in a low tone: "They said you'd been stopping out all night."

"Uncle knows I didn't," said Caroline, beginning to tremble. "What beasts men are! Didn't uncle tell them?"

"Oh yes; he told 'em right enough. But he come home in a fine rage, I can tell you. He said he wasn't going to have no more of it: and I believe he would have gone straight to Miss Temple—only she has always behaved very decent to us, and he didn't like to make mischief, seeing she is so set on the feller."

"Why didn't uncle come to me?" said Caroline. "Why didn't you make him, aunt?"

Mrs. Creddle shook her head. "When you know as much about men as I do——"

"But what was his reason?" asked Caroline.

"He said it was no good saying anything to you, because when a lass gets feller-fond there's no doing nothing with her. He said he couldn't use the strap to you now, but he wasn't going to have any lass belonging to him talked about in that way."

There was a moment's silence. "Did uncle tell you what Mr. Wilson said?" Then she threw up her head. "But I expect he threatened to go for uncle."

"Go for him!" echoed Mrs. Creddle. "Not he. He only wanted to get away and not have a scandal in the place."

"I don't believe that," said Caroline. "Uncle can say what he likes, but I don't believe that."

"It's true, my lass," said Mrs. Creddle kindly. "I ran along to tell you now, for fear you should come across Wilson or your uncle before you knew. He promised on his honour to have naught no more to do with you."

"Did he?" said Caroline, her blazing eyes very near to her aunt's in that tiny place. "Then he is a day too late for the fair—and uncle too. You may tell uncle that. I haven't seen Mr. Wilson for ten days or more, and I'll never enter uncle's house again as long as I live."

"You mustn't talk like that, honey," said Mrs. Creddle. "Uncle took it to heart because he thinks such a lot of you. But you'll soon find some nice young feller in your own station of life next time: don't go hankering after a gentleman, my dear. You would never get one of the best sort, and the other sort's no good to you." She sighed. "But you always had high notions, Carrie, though I don't know where you get them from. I suppose they're going about." With that Mrs. Creddle opened the little door of the pay-box, and let in a blast of air that nearly blew her hat from her head; then she hurried down the wind-swept road in order to get her husband's dinner ready before that already irritated breadwinner should return.

But Caroline sat down again on her chair and threw open the little window so that the salt air could blow across her face. She did not want to cry, because at any minute some one might want to come through the barrier; but after a minute or two she had no fear of that. She began to burn so with outraged pride that she could not yet feel the deeper ache of wounded love. Over and over again the words formed of themselves on the surface of the whirling storm in her mind: "I aren't *going* to give in! I aren't *going* to be pitied!"

Then a member of the promenade band came along, fighting with the gale, obliged to fetch some music which he had left in the hall the night before. "Wild morning! Can't say I'm sorry we close to-morrow," he said.

Caroline answered him, but he still lingered, though he had never taken any particular notice of her before, and did not know why he felt inclined to stop to-day. He suddenly felt that Caroline was interesting, though he was not actually aware of that odd shining of the spirit through the flesh—like a lamp in an alabaster vase—which was characteristic of Caroline in moments of supreme, passionate emotion. All he thought was, that there was something unusual about the girl, and that he was sorry he had not noticed it before.

Still, as a decent married man with a wife and children, he took such pleasures as talking to the girl on the promenade in strict moderation, so very soon he went off with his mackintosh flapping.

A few minutes later Lillie came to relieve guard, her woollen tam o' shanter wet and her front hair blown out of curl.

"I've had about enough of this," she said. "I'm going to find another job before next summer."

"Oh, I expect your job will be putting your boy's slippers before the fire and getting his tea ready," said Caroline, still speaking from the very top of her thoughts—as careful as if she were treading on very thin ice, not to risk the depths.

The prospective bride giggled, gratified, and Caroline went out; but the next minute she was startled to hear Lillie call shrilly from the little window: "Carrie! Carrie! You've forgotten your umbrella, and on a day like this! You must be in love!"

Caroline took the umbrella, but said nothing; she was at the end of her powers.

Chapter XX
Levelling

When Caroline reached the Cottage she was surprised to see the front door standing wide open, for the storm swept full across the garden from the south now that the privet hedge was taken up. The next moment Laura came out, her face almost ghastly under the tan, and she put her hand on Caroline's arm.

"There's bad news," she said, and paused. Caroline's thoughts flew to Godfrey, and her heart missed a beat. Then Laura went on again: "Miss Ethel has had a fall. I am afraid she is very seriously ill indeed. She was carrying a china pail downstairs and it was too heavy for her."

Caroline stared into Laura's face, forgetting Godfrey. "Oh, Miss Laura! I know what it was. I forgot to empty the pail, and she was doing it. If she dies I have killed her. It's my fault. It's all my fault!"

"Oh no; nothing of the sort," said Laura, a little impatiently, for she had no clue to Caroline's previously over-wrought condition. "The doctor thinks the fall was owing to some sort of seizure."

Then they entered the house together, and as they crossed the hall Wilson came out from the sitting-room; but beyond a grave good morning to Caroline he said nothing, passing at once to the coat lobby to fetch his hat and coat.

Caroline hesitated a moment, not quite knowing what to do: then she went into the kitchen. Her meal was put ready on the table just as Miss Ethel had left it, and when Caroline saw the piece of meat and the cold tart and bread so neatly arranged for her by those hands so long unaccustomed to manual labour, she felt her lips begin to tremble. It was hard. Poor Miss Ethel! Poor Miss Ethel! If only she had remembered to empty that pail! If only—— And all at once she was seized by a passion of weeping which she could neither stop nor control. But it was not really for Miss Ethel—it was for that, terrible blow to her love and pride which came before.

Then Miss Panton came into the kitchen with a hot-water bottle; so Caroline sprang up, choking back her sobs. "Here, let me fill that, Miss Panton!" As she went to the fireplace where there was a kettle boiling, she added in a low voice: "How is Miss Ethel now?"

"The doctor says she is unconscious," answered Miss Panton, also speaking in the unnatural voice which people use at such a time. "It was a blessing the man happened to be laying sods where the privet hedge used to be, or I don't know what Mrs. Bradford would have done. She ran out to him, and he fetched the woman who lives in that new house over the hedge. It seems she was a trained nurse before she married."

"I hope Miss Ethel didn't know. She hated that house being built," said Caroline.

"I don't think she knew; but it wouldn't have mattered to her, poor dear," said Miss Panton. "I suppose that's why it is so dreadful to feel that nothing matters—it always has a taste of death." She spoke from the deeps of her own experience, wise with what she had lived through; but the next second she turned uncertain again and thrust forth one of her copy-book maxims. "Yes, yes. Decessity makes strange bed-fellows."

Caroline fastened the hot-water bag. "I'll run upstairs with this," she said. "Then I shall see if there is anything else I can do."

"I am afraid there is dothing anyone can do," said Miss Panton, for her catarrh had come back with her nervous self-consciousness.

Mrs. Bradford came slowly downstairs into the hall, her big face congested with weeping. "Oh, Caroline!" she said.

But she could not say any more, and walked on into the sitting-room where the Vicar was already seated.

"Oh, Vicar: I'm afraid you are too late," she said, and began to weep afresh. "It's so dreadfully, dreadfully sudden."

"I came the moment Mr. Wilson told me. I chanced to be in the house," said the Vicar. He paused. "I wouldn't trouble too much about my being late, Mrs. Bradford. Miss Ethel did not leave things until now, you know. She was ready to meet her God."

"She is quite unconscious," said Mrs. Bradford. "At first she kept murmuring over and over: 'Everything's so different.—everything's so different.' But the doctor said it was probably what she was saying to herself when she fell. It meant nothing."

"Meant nothing!" It was Miss Panton's voice, which cut abruptly across their solemn conversation, startling them both; but she had again forgotten herself entirely. "You say it meant nothing—when she's dying of it."

"Of what? Of things being different!" said Laura, speaking from a corner of the room where she had intended to remain silent.

But some one had to break that terrible pause. For Miss Panton—Nanty—with all her silliness had spoken words which were to all of them like a search-light suddenly turned upon the inner secrets of the woman who was dying upstairs.

"Poor Ethel! I'm afraid so," said Mrs. Bradford. "It's true that she did take things to heart—about the new houses, and the hedge, and all the rest." But the next moment that blinding light was blurred in Mrs. Bradford's mind: "Of course I disliked the changes too—only I took them differently. I am sure they did not produce my sister's illness. Of course not." And she glanced at Miss Panton with heavy-eyed disfavour.

"I am afraid Miss Ethel dreaded the idea of leaving this house," said the Vicar.

"Yes, yes," said Mrs. Bradford. "You see, it was the only home my sister ever knew." And despite her real grief, she glanced up instinctively at Mr. Bradford's portrait, triumphing over the sister who lay upstairs.

"Some natures find these swift and tremendous changes harder to bear than others," said the Vicar. "But there is only one way for people like ourselves to take it, Mrs. Bradford. We must be kind, do the next job, and hold fast——"

Then he broke off, for the nurse was beckoning at the door; the end had come sooner than they expected.

Caroline drew down the blinds all over the house and then hovered about the hall in her coat and hat, not knowing whether to go back to the promenade or not. Lillie would want to leave, of course; but then she herself might be required here. At last Godfrey came through, but he did not seem real to her. She was so exhausted by her own emotion and by the shock of Miss Ethel's death, that she was actually indifferent to him for the moment.

"Do you think I ought to go for Aunt Creddle?" she said tonelessly. "They will want some one to help."

He did not answer at once, looking at her with a harassed expression, as if he scarcely was aware of what she said. He had a strained and haggard look which sat so oddly on his firm-fleshed, strong-featured face, but she knew it was not produced by grief for Miss Ethel. There was a little leap of the heart, then dull apathy again. Of course it was the money troubles which everybody seemed to know about——

She was about to repeat the question about Aunt Creddle, when Laura came out of the room, and Godfrey immediately said with an air of relief: "Oh, here is Miss Temple. She will be able to tell you better than I can."

Laura paused, and for a moment the two girls stared at each other—interrogating, blaming, excusing—what was it? Anyway, it was over in a flash. The next second Caroline felt it was all imagination, for Laura came forward as frankly as usual, though her kind eyes were a little swollen with tears.

"What a good idea, Miss Raby," she said. "Mrs. Creddle is such a comfortable person when one is in trouble. I'm sure Mrs. Bradford will be glad to have her."

"I'll come back as soon as I have let Lillie know, if there is anything I can do. I can easily get some other girl to take my place," said Caroline.

"No, thank you. Really, there is nothing you can do," said Laura. "You see, there is the nurse and Miss Panton, and myself; besides your aunt, if she comes. We should only run over each other."

Laura's voice was no less pleasant than before, but Caroline felt dismissed. The vague impression of that first, odd moment became startlingly vivid again. But even now she could not be sure that it was not all imagination—the effect of her own self-consciousness, after what had passed between herself and Laura's lover.

As she walked down the drive she saw the jobbing gardener had returned and was continuing to lay sods on the ground where the privet hedge had been. The thought passed through her mind that it looked like a new grave fresh sodded. Then she began to plan in her mind what she should say to Aunt Creddle, and to picture how that good-hearted woman would take it. At last she remembered her declaration only a few hours ago—could it be only a few hours ago?—that she would never enter Uncle Creddle's house again.

Now, it did not seem to matter. The heat of her pride and anger had died down and she began to see that her love for Godfrey was too deep to be destroyed by anger or even contempt. He had planted it in her heart and she must carry it about always. Neither of them by any act of theirs could take it away from her.

But she was not actively and vitally miserable. Her being was simply soaked in a dull unhappiness which made her quite indifferent to the healthy pricking of small annoyances, so that when Mr. and Mrs. Graham passed her with the barest of cold salutations, and never stopped to ask for news, even at this sad crisis, she did not care.

She was finding out the truth of what Miss Panton had said in the kitchen of the cottage—that every time a human being really feels it does not matter, he or she has a bitter foretaste of death, which is what makes this of all emotions the most truly sad.

Even when she reached Aunt Creddle's, whose words and exclamations fell about her ears like hail, she remained the same—delivering her message, then going on at once to take her place in the pay-box.

Lillie had already heard the news and was rather shocked that she should wish to remain. "Anybody can see you've been crying. Now, don't you think about me, Carrie. I don't mind stopping a bit."

"No, thanks, I'd rather be here. After all, it's my job. And they don't want me—there are plenty there without me," said Caroline.

But Lillie urged her at least to go somewhere and have a nice hot cup of tea and a rest, even if she were not needed at the Cottage; then at last departed, rebuffed and slightly irritated.

Caroline sat down on the chair; but she did not take up her knitting, though the rain now fell heavily, persistently, and fewer people than ever passed through the barrier. She remained there with her hands idle, her eyes fixed on the expanse of sea that stretched out before her, so full of buoyant life, the spray from the breakers blown back like smoke in the wind under the swiftly-moving grey clouds.

After a while the handful of people who had been listening to the concert in the hall came out into the rain, shouting remarks to each other above the gale. "Windiest place in England! Very bracing, though—too bracing for my taste!"

A little later members of the band scurrying back to their lodgings: then utter silence, but for the sound of the wind and sea. But just before Lillie was due back again the weather cleared a little—between majestic clouds sweeping along like galleons, appeared a stretch of pure blue sky.

Perhaps it was some association of childhood, some impression she had gained, then, from a hymn speaking of death; but that bright blue sky made her suddenly think with an acute vividness of the woman who was dead. Where was Miss Ethel? What was she doing now?

Caroline's eyes remained fixed on the blue, but her mind had gone searching into the unknown; she was really groping her way, for the first time, across the barriers that lie between this life and the life of the world to come. Her soul really was trying to follow the soul of one already on the other side. Thus, strangely, it was Miss Ethel—buffeted and overcome by change—who led Caroline to this first glimpse of the unchanging.

But these things do not become a conscious part of experience until long afterwards; so Caroline went home to her tea without knowing what had happened—only thinking rather more regretfully and kindly than before about Miss Ethel.

Chapter XXI
St. Martin's Summer

The storm gave place to still weather the day before Miss Ethel's funeral. But that was all now over, so was the Sunday morning sermon wherein the Vicar referred to the good works of the departed, and during which members of the congregation felt for their pocket-handkerchiefs who had not troubled to go near the Cottage for months, or perhaps years.

Though this had happened some days ago the fine weather still held, and Laura had persuaded Mrs. Bradford to come down to the now deserted promenade for a little change of scene. They sat silent on the long bench; Mrs. Bradford a little overdone in her heavy black clothes on such an unexpectedly warm morning, and Laura looking at a sea which once more broke in harmless little glittering waves on the firm sand. The storm had dashed the water right up to the sea-wall, washing away all traces of the Thorhaven season from that part of the shore, while on the promenade itself butterflies fluttered among the flower beds devastated by wind and rain. Far away down the beach, she saw the donkeys which had been ridden by children all the summer to the hootings of donkey boys, but they now plodded sedately with gravel in panniers on their backs up the cliff path, just as their ancestors had done for centuries past. It seemed really as if some power too immense for constant interference had grown suddenly tired of bands, visitors, tents, buckets and spades, and had swept them all away with a gesture, leaving only the stretch of shore; much as it was before Thorhaven existed, and as it would be when Thorhaven was under the sea like the other village beyond, which coast erosion had taken.

Perhaps Laura may have found this contrast between permanence and fleetingness depressing; anyway, her face was sad as she sat quietly there, looking in front of her. After a while she turned round to look inland, where the hall and the café and the pay-box were all shuttered and closed— already appearing somehow desolate. Then Mrs. Bradford, having regained her breath, felt that gratitude made a remark necessary.

"Your loss is my gain, my dear," she said. "If you had not put off your wedding again, you would not be here to keep me company. When is it to be now?"

The blood deepened in Laura's face right up to the roots of her hair, but she smiled and answered easily: "Oh, no exact time has been fixed."

"Ah, well; I daresay you are right. You can't enjoy anything—even getting married—when you are in bad health. I was told the postponement might have something to do with Godfrey's financial difficulties," Mrs. Bradford added, "but I felt sure there was nothing in that report." Still she glanced curiously at the girl by her side.

"No, it was not that." Laura paused, then went on: "Every business man who is making his way occasionally takes on more business than he has capital for. But I am sure he will get through all right. It was only temporary."

"I'm glad of that, I'm sure," said Mrs. Bradford. Then she lowered her voice confidentially: "But if I were you, I should see that my own money was securely tied up. Godfrey may be a Wilson, but he is human. I know poor Ethel would not have said this to you, because she always thought so much of the family. I don't blame her—poor Ethel!—but being married naturally gives one a wider view." And having thus triumphed over Miss Ethel, even in her grave, Mrs. Bradford relapsed into silence. Laura seemed equally inclined to sit quiet, so nothing more was said for a considerable time. At last three girls came walking briskly along the promenade, stimulating a further effort at conversation.

"I'm glad Caroline has decided to stay with us until our things are sold," said Mrs. Bradford.

"Yes. She has been very obliging," said Laura. Then Mrs. Bradford's thoughts went evenly inward again. "I have arranged to keep my own chair. The proprietress of the boarding-house at Scarborough has been very obliging about having it placed in a corner out of the draught. They like a permanent boarder who is well recommended, and I shall be quite comfortable so long as I have my own chair in a nice corner, and my book and my knitting. You see, the sale of the house and furniture will enable me to take a good room on the first floor. I have no doubt I shall be all right there"—she paused—"as right as I can be now, that is to say," she added, her lip trembling.

During the silence which followed, the three girls passed once more—heads erect and neatly-shod feet stepping lightly on the hard path. Mrs. Bradford looked after them with a sort of dull aversion. "Two of those girls' mothers were in service. Why aren't they?"

"I suppose they prefer other employment," said Laura.

"They'd be far better off in domestic service. Now they are only doing what men can do. But men can't do what the girls' mothers used to do," said Mrs. Bradford. "I can't see that they are doing any good in the world at all."

"Can't you?" Laura hesitated a moment, piecing together her own thoughts. "Well, do you know, Mrs. Bradford—I didn't think of it before— but I really do believe girls like those are achieving something rather wonderful, after all. I believe they are reaching up to a stage of manners and speech which will soon cause them to merge with the girls of our own class, so that you can't feel any difference. Then we shall get the real equality which people are always talking about. They're doing it the right way, too, levelling up, not levelling down."

"Oh! Is that how you look at Caroline?" said Mrs. Bradford.

Laura waited for a moment. "Yes," she said then, "Caroline is one of those I mean."

Mrs. Bradford relapsed into silence again, and they sat so for a long time. Then Laura rose abruptly: "Oh, here are the Grahams! Do let us move on."

Mrs. Bradford also rose, impelled by the urgency of her companion's tone, but wondering in her dull way what it was that made Laura turn so red, and seem so anxious to get away all of a sudden. Surely Laura could not have quarrelled with the Grahams? Then being very curious—like the majority of stupid people—she sat obstinately down again. "I must have a word or two with Mr. and Mrs. Graham," she said. "They have been so kind. But don't you wait, Laura, unless you like. I dare say you have other things to do."

"Oh no, I am not busy this morning: besides, it is too late to do anything now before lunch." And she also sat down again.

The Grahams came up and immediately began to explain in subdued tones about Mr. Graham's sore throat, which was so bad on the day of the funeral that his wife absolutely threatened to lock the front door if he attempted to attend. It was equally unfortunate that one of Mrs. Graham's prostrating sick headaches obliged her husband to forbid her paying that last token of respect and affection to dear Miss Ethel.

Mrs. Bradford murmured a vague reply, wiping her eyes, and saying that the cross of early chrysanthemums was very beautiful—it was nice of them to remember that poor Ethel liked chrysanthemums. Then after a pause she mentioned the delicious fruit and potted meats which the Grahams had sent her almost daily, for indeed they were very kind when it did not hurt them.

Laura said little, but the occasion was not one for discussing her affairs, so that denoted nothing; and very soon the Grahams went off, without satisfying Mrs. Bradford's curiosity in any way.

Mrs. Bradford's legs retained the same inability to do anything their owner did not wish as had distinguished them during Miss Ethel's lifetime, so towards sunset she sent Caroline to do various errands in the village.

As the girl went along, she had on her right the old grey tower of the church standing with a sort of noble repose against the red and orange sunset. It made her think of Miss Ethel, laid to rest in the old churchyard in the middle of the village—among friends and neighbours of her youth. The churchyard was now only used by those who had the old family graves there, so that Caroline had never been at a funeral exactly like Miss Ethel's before, and those in the new cemetery had not made the same impression on her mind.

But her attention was diverted now by the sight of the carrier with his trolley, who had brought her box to the Cottage that day in the spring. And as she began to run after him, her flying figure was caught here and there by the glow of the sunset, giving her a slight momentary resemblance to the nymph on fire that Wilson's fancy had once seen in her.

Wilson, himself, may even have been reminded of this as he stood looking after her; but he turned up the road leading to Laura Temple's, and Caroline remained unaware that he had been anywhere near.

She had a long run before the carrier heard her calling: then he pulled up his old white horse and waited at the top of the little hill, the air about them seeming almost iridescent with the gold and red of the autumn sunset shining through it.

"Here you are again, then," he said as she came up. "Where do you want your box moved to this time? You see, you stopped on at the Cottage, after all."

"I'm not going yet—not for another fortnight." She was panting slightly, a little out of breath. "I want you to take a typewriter for me to Mr. Wilson's lodgings. It's one he left at the Cottage for me to practise on."

"All right. I'll call round to-morrow," he replied.

"Oh! I do wish you could come to-night," she said. "I particularly want it to go back to-night."

The carrier laughed good-naturedly, looking down at her. "Oh, that's it, is it?" he said. "Well, you're in the right on it. One lass is enough for any man. Gee-up." And he shouted back as he went: "I'll call round in an hour or so."

Caroline stood still in the road as he jolted round out of sight, forgetting to move, her bodily sensations all swamped by the tumult of her mind. How dare he say such a thing! she said to herself; then she burst forth, aloud: "I aren't going to have it. I *aren't* going to have it!"

But behind all that, she felt the iron touch of reality. Life was not to be as she wanted it, just because she was herself—as she had felt in the past. No matter how she might rebel, she'd *got* to "have it." The people in Thorhaven must pity her or laugh at her as they liked: she could not prevent them from destroying the steps she had hewn with such careful pains on the side of that steep hill which led to everything she desired. With all her fun and easy friendliness she had always kept herself a little "nice"—a little carefully unsmirched—holding her head up among the other girls—— And now they had the laugh of her. Now, she thought—standing there, digging her finger-nails into her palms—now they'd giggle and talk about her as they did about all those others who had been made fools of and left in the lurch. And she could not get away from it all. Despite her fine talk about never entering Uncle Creddle's house again, she had found that it would be literally impossible to live in Flodmouth on what she earned at first, and she would be obliged to lodge with Aunt Creddle, going in and out by train every day.

Suddenly, the thought swept over her of how she had gloried in the idea of travelling with the other girls who were off to places of business in Flodmouth—all so neat, and nicely dressed, and so independent. Now that was spoilt, like everything else.

Then the sudden hooting of a motor-bicycle caused her to start aside, and Wilf careered past—cap correctly poised, slim young body bent forward. The next moment, he swerved round with a dash and swirl, shouting out:

"Hello! hello! You'll be getting run down one of these days!" But it was to show his new motor-bicycle, and what he had gained by her "turning him down," as well as what she had lost.

Caroline was conscious of his triumphant attitude, though she only felt a sort of incredulous wonder that she could ever have thought of him as a lover. It seemed, somehow, to have happened in another life, so far off it appeared from her present experiences.

After that two girls whom she knew passed, laughing and talking together on the other side of the road, and she immediately felt sure that they were making fun of her. No doubt it was all over the town that she had been "carrying on" with Wilson—a man just about to be married to Miss Temple, whom everybody respected and liked. There would be no pity there—only contempt. So she called out "good night" and went on as fast as she could, fancying what the girls were saying to each other. "Well, *I* wouldn't have done such a thing! And I never reckoned to be as particular as Carrie Raby. But pride will have a fall——"

She could almost hear them say it as she hurried on, her ambition as well as her love so deeply wounded that she could scarcely bear herself. Revolting, fighting—having to find out with exasperated agony like every one else that those who fight against destiny only hurt themselves. But as she passed the short street leading to the promenade a strong current of sea-air blew down it and she turned her hot face towards the breeze, looking up towards the pay-box which stood silent and deserted in the fading light. It took on for her now that strange quality which belongs to places where we have felt a great deal—as if the walls had absorbed some of the currents of emotion which had been given out there. She both loved the little wooden erection, and longed never to see it again. Beyond it, the Flamborough lights swung out across the sea: white—white—red. How unhappy life was! And contempt did not kill love, as she had always understood from the novels in the pretty paper covers which she liked to read so much. It had killed trust; but the ache in her went on just the same, even though Godfrey had been threatened by Uncle Creddle with a big stick, and had shown such a cowardly anxiety to escape a row.

She drew in deep breaths of the salt air—cold, invigorating as it always was here after sunset on the warmest days; and all her mind was bent on despising him as he deserved. She tried to put her contempt into words, so as to make it more real. "He's no good. I'm well rid of him. I wouldn't have anything to do with him now, not if he were to crawl after me on his hands and knees from here to Flamborough."

But the silence of the evening gave back an answer which she was obliged to hear in her heart; and she told herself, though with less certainty: "I *won't* care; I *will* end by not caring. He's not worth it."

But at last she did manage to flick the raw place until she was really bitter against him. For the sudden thought came to her that he dare not have behaved to a girl of his own sort in the same way as he had done to her. It was because he looked down on her that he could do it.

Then she saw the two girls coming her way down the road again, and hurried up the side street in order to escape them. But they followed, evidently going to the promenade, so she turned down to the shore where she was certain of being alone at this season and this hour. As she went along, a most vivid sense of this waste of her youth's bright happiness came across her. "I *will* forget him! I aren't *going* to be made miserable just by falling in love," she said to herself, half sobbing—a little figure running along through the twilight by the edge of the sea like a leaf driven by the wind, flinging defiance at the god of love whom no change can displace.

Chapter XXII
Morning

It was two days later, and Caroline was going down to cash a cheque for Mrs. Bradford. There had been a slight touch of frost in the night, and the atmosphere was so rarified this morning that every object seemed to meet the eye with equal distinctness—with the effect, somehow, of a Dutch painting. A little black dog jumping up excitedly outside the fishmonger's, a woman in the doorway of the little toy-shop taking down a bundle of wooden spades, a red-faced farmer getting out of his trap at the bank—all looked equally clear, lacking the usual hazy effect of the damp air. It was partly for this reason, perhaps, that Caroline felt as if everybody were pressing round her, and trying to read her thoughts. Though the toy-shop woman called out a pleasant "good morning," after her habit, Caroline thought she peered curiously from behind her grove of spades, and that she was no doubt wondering what it felt like to be made the "talk of the place"—especially by a gentleman who allowed stout, middle-aged Mr. Creddle to threaten horse-whipping with impunity. Then in going past the fish-shop, the very cod seemed to turn a contemptuous, lack-lustre eye upon her, as if they also said to each other: "There goes the girl who was made a fool of by a man who never really meant to marry her."

But it was the worst when she caught sight of the hoarding on the little Picture Hall. For suddenly the phrase which she had seen there on the film flashed across her mind with such vividness that it seemed to be written in dancing, bright letters across the sunshiny street: "I swear I want to marry you."

She felt dizzy, then it passed. It was true enough, of course. Men did always say that, as Aunt Creddle had told her. She was only one of the millions of silly girls so easily deceived. And she went down the street, feeling that from every eye streamed out a baleful ray which reached and hurt the sore place in her heart.

At last she came to the bank; and the farmer was there at the counter, pushing his notes across grudgingly—as does the man of all nations who has wrung his hard living out of the soil. "I hate these no-ates," he was saying. "They do-an't seem like money. But I doubt they'll last my da-ay."

His drawl seemed to go in and out of Caroline's thoughts, soothing her while she waited; then she heard a door open beyond the counter and saw Laura come forth, attended by the bank-manager, and wearing a jaded, excited look, as if she had been through a difficult interview in which she had at last come off triumphant. On catching sight of Caroline she flushed deeply, hesitating for a second, then coming forward with hand outstretched. "Oh, I was wanting to see you, Miss Raby."

Caroline wondered why Laura should look like that on unexpectedly meeting her, if this were so; but the farmer went out and his place at the counter was now clear. Laura, however, followed her, saying in a low tone: "Is Mrs. Bradford at home this morning?"

"No," said Caroline, "she has gone to see Mrs. Graham."

"Ah, I thought so." She paused. "Are you going straight home?"

"Yes, at least, I have only one other errand," said Caroline. With that she turned to the man behind the counter who was waiting to transact her business, and Laura went out of the bank.

Caroline walked home, thinking once or twice about the incident, for Laura's manner seemed odd if she only wanted to know whether Mrs. Bradford were at home or not. Then about an hour later, when she was near a front window, she chanced to see Laura coming up the drive. So going to the door; she said at once: "I'm sorry, but Mrs. Bradford has not come in yet. Do you care to leave a message?"

As Laura stood there hesitating, that odd mixture of maturity and a sort of girlish angularity in her appearance became unusually marked. "No—no message. I—I think I will just come in."

"But I am afraid Mrs. Bradford may be some time," said Caroline.

Laura looked at her as if seeking something in her face, then repeated awkwardly: "Oh! I think I will just come in."

So Caroline led the way to the sitting-room, but just as she was about to go, Laura said quickly: "I suppose you like the idea of working at an office?"

"Oh yes; I think it will be all right, thank you," said Caroline, moving on towards the door all the time. She did not want to stay in the same room with this girl who was to marry Godfrey. Let them marry and be happy, so far as she was concerned; but she did not want to have anything to do with either of them again.

Then she went through the door, but before she was across the hall she heard Laura's voice raised on a sort of high, breathless note calling after her: "Don't—don't go, yet. I—we so seldom have a chat. This—this must have been a most trying time for you."

Caroline went back and stood just within the door, her small face pale and rather severe. What did this girl want of her? For she could see that there was something behind those halting words which Laura felt either afraid or ashamed to say. She would not help by a single word. No, not though the kind brown eyes began to distress her a little, like those of a dog with a hurt paw.

"I suppose office work is really what you like best?" said Laura nervously. "You think you will really enjoy it? You"—she drew a breath and plunged, as it were—"you have no idea of getting married at present?"

"No," said Caroline, speaking with fair composure, though her own nerves began to quiver and she breathed rather quickly. For this was what Laura had come for, then! She had heard tales and wanted to find out if they were true.

Well—let her! For one second a great temptation assailed Caroline. She stood there in the doorway, with the power of happiness or unhappiness in her hands, knowing perfectly well that she had only to tell the actual, unvarnished truth as it had actually happened for Godfrey's chance of a rich wife, and Laura's chance of a probably successful marriage to vanish in less time than you could open and shut the door.

But the next moment it was all over. She knew, with a just pride, that she could never do a mean trick like that: it was not in her. When the room, which had gone a little dim, grew clear again, she heard herself continuing, as if it were somebody else: "I'm sure I shall enjoy being on my own. I'd rather keep myself than be dependent on any man. You can do as you like. It's better than getting married."

"But nothing is better than marriage with the right man," said Laura. She was still looking intently at Caroline; still seeming all the time to have something behind her words which hovered but remained unspoken. Then, suddenly her eyes filled with tears.

Caroline looked away, perplexed and troubled. "I'm afraid Mrs. Bradford may not be in for some time."

Laura rose in a hesitating fashion. "Do you think so? Well, I suppose I had better go. Mrs. Bradford will be glad when the sale is over. She will be happier in a boarding-house at Scarborough."

They were at the front door now; and to avoid looking at each other they both glanced at the man who was wheeling a barrow-load of building implements in from the field across the place where the privet hedge used to be.

"I suppose that is for the improvements to the Cottage?" said Laura, who seemed as if she could not go and yet did not really want to stay.

"Yes. They begin altering the outside buildings before the sale," said Caroline; but all the time she was asking within herself: "What is it? What is it?"

Again they looked at the man, who was now trudging back over the newly-laid sods.

"Poor Miss Ethel!" said Laura. "She would not have liked that, would she?"

Caroline shook her head, not speaking—it was all so curiously far off from what they were both thinking about that words only seemed to echo from a distance. "There have to be changes," she said at last, growing afraid of the pause lest it should imply too much.

"Well, Miss Ethel always hated change," said Laura. Then her expression began to alter curiously under Caroline's eyes—becoming charged, as it were, with an inner radiance that shone right through the outer dullness, or embarrassment, or sadness—whatever there might be. "At any rate, she has gone where things are certain."

Caroline's heart beat fast with the sudden impact of discovery. Laura, too, then! They were both just like people hanging on to a spar in a rough sea and hoping to be thrown on shore at last. That was what life was, even when you were going to be married to the man of your choice. But the expression of Laura's face—or was it that thought of a rough sea?—had in some way brought back that time in the pay-box after Miss Ethel's death, when Caroline herself had looked up at the blue sky breaking through the grey. Once more she tried to grope across the barrier between the seen and the unseen.

What was there after all? Then a line of one of those Sunday-school hymns floated across her mind—"Oh, Thou that changest not"—And the thought of Miss Ethel on the stairs with that heavy pail in her hand.

But the thoughts passed so quickly that Laura had not noticed the pause. "I like to fancy Miss Ethel in a place where things don't change. It makes you think, when somebody you know goes——" And Caroline saw Laura felt the same; was drawn more closely in touch with this eternity to which Miss Ethel had just gone over.

Then a man over in the field shouted loudly to his mate. Both girls glanced, half startled, in that direction, and when they looked at each other again the mental atmosphere had quite altered.

"Well, I must be going," said Laura.

But it was still so evident she had left something unsaid, that Caroline remained half-consciously expectant in the doorway. And a few steps down the drive Laura did suddenly stop short, pause a moment and return with quick, nervous steps. "Oh, by the way, I suppose you won't know that my engagement with Mr. Wilson is broken off?"

For a moment—an age—Caroline's throat seemed to dry up, and she felt like a person in a nightmare struggling to make a sound which will not come. Then, out of all the turmoil of questions, fears, emotions that Laura's words had caused to seethe within her, she was only able to bring to the surface: "I—I didn't know."

"No?" Laura paused. "Well, you'll tell Mrs. Bradford I have been——" And she hurried away down the drive; but she had not yet lost that air of having left something unsaid which she had come on purpose to say.

Caroline could see her near the gate, then paused a moment as at the approach of voices; and the next minute Mr. and Mrs. Graham came in, accompanying Mrs. Bradford. Their attitudes were most plainly visible to Caroline in the doorway, though she could not hear what was said; Mrs. Bradford solidly engrossed in her own importance as a mourner—Mr. Graham bending forward to speak to Laura, conciliatory, voluble; and Laura herself unresponsive.

Caroline gave a last look at them before going indoors to take the potatoes from the fire; and as she did so, she experienced one of those sudden, blindingly clear moments of intuition common to almost every one, in which the processes of fact, argument, reason are all skipped, and the knowledge is there, full blown. She knew perfectly well that Mr. and Mrs. Graham had felt it their solemn duty to inform Laura—with the best intentions—of what was being said about Godfrey Wilson and the girl on the promenade.

But before she had time to turn away the group dissolved, Laura going on alone, while Mrs. Bradford and Mrs. Graham came up the drive. The picture bit like acid into her mind. The three coming up the path; the clear sky; the man with the barrow wheeling cement over the forlorn dismantled part of the garden where the privet hedge had been.

But in the kitchen, while she was taking the potatoes from the steamer, her face suddenly flushed crimson. "I aren't going to be frightened," she murmured to herself. "I aren't going to care what anybody says. She would never break off her engagement because of a bit of scandal. She's not that sort. They'll be married, all right."

Beneath her defiance, however, Caroline was terribly afraid. She sub-consciously so dreaded the agony she must endure if he did come after her again and she had to send him away. For that was what she would do. Never for one second did she waver in her determination to have no more to do with a man who could behave as he had done. She couldn't help loving him, but she could help trusting him with her life.

Mrs. Bradford appeared, black and bulky in the kitchen doorway. "Oh, Caroline——" And her voice, though heavy and rather husky, put the same immeasurable distance between Caroline and every Wilson in the world as Miss Ethel's clear tones, speaking the same words, had always done. "I am expecting Mr. Wilson on business after tea. Will you show him into the breakfast-room if you have not gone out when he comes?"

Caroline murmured acquiescence, angry to feel herself blushing; and when she looked up Mrs. Bradford's little eyes were fixed on her with the insatiable curiosity of the dull; so she looked steadily down again at the bowl of potatoes. After a pause that seemed very long, she heard the pad-pad-pad of a heavy, elderly woman's walk sounding along the passage.

Mrs. Bradford, waiting for her lunch, also looked at the wheel-marks left by the passing of the workman's barrow over the place where the privet hedge used to be. She might not like it, but she was without that fiery hatred of change which did actually release Miss Ethel's spirit for its escape to certainty.

Chapter XXIII
On the Shore

Mrs. Bradford was timid about being alone in the house after sunset since her sister's death, so Caroline usually went out between tea and early supper. On this occasion she hurried off directly tea was over, in her anxiety to avoid a possible meeting with Godfrey. She did not even wait to go upstairs and change her dress, but kept on the old blouse and skirt she had been wearing beneath her overall, put on an old garden hat and ran down the drive, fearing all the time to hear Mrs. Bradford calling from the doorway.

However, she reached the road in safety, thankful that there was now no chance of being obliged to usher in Godfrey with Mrs. Bradford's dull rather malicious gaze fixed on her. But even while she waited a second, out of breath, she caught sight of his figure coming along the road from the town, and hurried on again towards the cliff top. There was the bench on which she had sat that moonlight night with Godfrey, when it seemed to her that they could love each other for ever just the same, no matter what might divide them. She had been filled then with the exultation which is so difficult to distinguish at the time from happiness—which seems so independent of human accident—a joy never to be assailed by common experience.

But all that had gone. Now she was going down the rough, muddy path on the side of the clay cliff—slipping, making her shoes and skirt dirty, grasping at the wiry grass as she slipped and not caring—simply because she wanted to escape any chance of meeting the same man who had inspired those wonderful emotions. The contrast seemed to hit a blow on her heart, even though she was not going to let it hurt her any more. But at last she reached the bottom, and stood for a moment to rest.

The sea, heaving with a strong ground-swell, reflected the pale blue of the sky in millions of pools of light on the dun-coloured surface. She was not conscious of looking at it, but she had a feeling of freshness and consolation—of freedom from herself. The truth was that, without knowing it, she had made a friend of the sea. She had done so during all those hours in the pay-box on the promenade when she endured that hard spiritual experience which turns people from children into men and women—and the sea remains faithful.

After resting a moment or two she walked on, her path skirting the wet sea-weed which showed that there had been heavy weather outside the bay.

The brown streamers had blue lights on them like the sea and the sand was firm and hard. A thick froth churned up from the deeps rested among the sea-weed, or blew along the shore in front of her before the south-easterly wind.

She inhaled the smell of fresh sea-weed—not exactly noticing it, but with her senses influenced by it, as a person's may be by the heavy scent of roses on a June evening. Less than ever was she going to give in because she had to do without love. There were plenty of things in life besides love——

Then, as if in answer to that defiance, she saw part of a man's shadow thrown by the westering sun on the sand before her. She swerved sharp round—not startled—not afraid; but filled with an extraordinary fury against Godfrey which may have been partly caused by these emotions.

"How dare you come creeping up after me on the sand like that?" she said. "Which way are you going? Tell me, and then I'll go the other."

He looked down at her with amusement and ardour in his glance; but all the same he bore the marks of some storm only just over in the strained lines of his face, and in the marks of sleeplessness under his eyes.

"You won't get rid of me so easily as that," he said. "I have come here to talk things out with you, and I mean to do it."

She turned back towards the promenade. "Of course, I can't prevent you walking with me if you will," she answered. But it was because she felt that her curiosity might betray her that she desperately slammed the door of opportunity in his face by adding: "I suppose you know you are safe here to worry me as much as you like. You won't come across Uncle Creddle on the sands."

"Your uncle——" He was rather thick-skinned and flushed seldom, but he did so now, growing crimson to the edge of the cap pulled down over his forehead. "Oh! I see. So you actually believed I was afraid. Turn round!" He took her arm and made her face him. "Now! Do I look as if I should be afraid to fight old Creddle?" She obstinately refused to answer, and he went on, still holding her: "You know I should not. I was thinking of you, and you only. Do you realize what people say about a girl when her nearest male relative breaks, or even tries to break a big stick over her lover's back? Well, I wasn't going to have anything of that sort said about you, Carrie."

"You were very thoughtful about my reputation all of a sudden," said Caroline. She paused, but the words had to come. "It was not because you wanted to keep any talk from getting to Miss Laura's ears, I suppose?"

The question was a sneer, but it was there, all the same; she had had to ask it. And now her whole being hung trembling on the answer, though she was no less grimly resolved than before to have done with a man whom she could not trust. But now he did not reply; and that burning urge of curiosity made Caroline go on—against better judgment, intention, pride: "Does she know?"

He released Caroline's arm at once and walked on. "Let us leave her out of the discussion," he said stiffly. "I was just about to tell you that our engagement is broken off."

But Caroline could not understand—any more than the majority of women—the feeling which makes a decent man reluctant to discuss an old love with a new one, and she was now easily able to speak as coldly as she wished. "I've heard that piece of news," she said.

He turned sharp round. "Why, who told you? It only happened last night."

"Miss Laura told me," she answered.

"What more did she tell you?" he asked quickly.

"Nothing."

He looked away from her to the sea without replying, and this was her chance to walk away, if she had wished; but there was still that question which she must have answered.

"Has Miss Laura heard anything about us? Was that why the engagement was broken off?"

He waited a moment. "No," he said. "After all, you have a right to know that you had nothing to do with it. Nothing. She had never heard a word about you and me until I told her myself; and that was after our engagement was broken off."

"Then why did you———?" She paused, so filled with all sorts of conflicting desires and emotions—longing to know, and yet passionately telling herself it didn't matter to her—that she had lost all certainty in herself, and her voice came sharp and tremulous.

"She simply threw me over," he said at last. "Found out she didn't like the idea of married life, though she was very fond of me. I suppose there are women like that in every civilized community. No doubt if she were a Roman Catholic she would be a nun, and she would be a good one. She's good all through. I realize that, in spite of what has happened."

Caroline looked at him as he faced the sea in the strong light—at his heavy features, his broadly set figure, his whole air of knowledge and virility and strength. Then the words fluttered up into her throat without any volition of her own: "Oh, you well may think her good! You well may!"

For in that moment she guessed what Laura had come to tell her but had not been able to say after all. That heavenly kindness of Laura's was actually deep enough and real enough to make her spare her lover the knowledge of how he had wounded her. It was clear enough that she—who always seemed so easy and simple—had detected the first little change in him when he became attracted to Caroline. So she had put off her wedding to make sure, and she had become sure.

Caroline opened her lips to say with passion: "Can't you *see* what she did it for?" But before the words left her lips, there came into her mind a memory of Laura's face as it looked when she left the door of the Cottage, which was so vivid as to be almost an illusion. Now she knew what the anxious, uncertain gaze of those brown eyes into her own had really meant.

Laura had been trying to say all the time: "Don't tell him! don't tell him!" But the complexities involved had been too great, when it came to the point, for anything to be actually said.

Caroline waited to get back her self-command, stirred by a sudden loyalty to her own sex which made her long to pierce his masculine obtuseness— to show him what Laura had sacrificed and what he had missed. And as he watched her, he wondered once more at the quality of aloofness—of something fresh and cool despite her passion—which had caused him to think of a nymph on fire when he first held her in his arms.

"Well?" he said at last. "It's all right now, isn't it?"

She shook her head. "I'm not going to begin that all over again," she said rather drearily. "You made me look silly once, but you won't have a chance a second time. So long as you thought you might marry Miss Laura, you were afraid of the talk and kept out of my way. Now she has turned you down, you come after me again. I don't know why. Just for your own fun, I suppose. You can't deny you avoided me."

"No." He stood with his hands thrust deep into his pockets. "I don't. But I was in a devil of a hole, Caroline. I was engaged to marry a good girl, and a nice girl, and shortly after the wedding day was fixed I did a thing which only a cad would have done." He paused, Caroline gazing at him with wide eyes. Then he went on: "I borrowed a large sum of money from her."

"Is that all?" breathed Caroline. "I don't see what difference that made."

"Don't you? Well, perhaps not—but any man would," he answered. "I was faced with ruin unless I could tide things over, and I couldn't take the money and be philandering with another girl at the same time."

"You didn't seem to hold those views until the last week or two," she said.

"I had not borrowed the money before," he said shortly. "Though I knew well enough I was not doing the square thing there, either by you or her."

She looked at him with a keen, set, impersonal intentness in her gaze which he could not understand. "Then you are sure she does not care enough for you to marry you? She threw you over because she wanted to stop single?"

"No doubt of that," he said with a sort of rueful conviction. "Though, of course, being the girl she is, she was frightfully upset at the idea of behaving badly to me. As a matter of fact, she seemed so distressed during the whole interview that I couldn't help feeling ashamed of myself. I couldn't let her reproach herself so acutely; I had to tell her I—I wasn't broken-hearted."

"She would wonder why, didn't she?" said Caroline, in a tone which he could not understand.

"Yes," he answered. "So I told her."

"What did you say?"

He waited a moment, looking down at the slim figure outlined darkly against the immense radiance of the sea. But he did not touch her. This was a different thing indeed from that hot wooing on the top of the cliff.

"I told her," he answered bluntly, at last, "that I was in love with you and wanted to marry you."

"And she——?" Caroline did not respond any more than that; incredibly, to him, she was still thinking about Laura—— And he stood looking at her with the same odd mixture of curiosity and desire which had all along marked his pursuit of her, though beneath it there was now something deeper, more human, more permanent. He wanted to know—— But even when he did know, she would be his—his to take care of and fight for and help up in the world.

At last he gave the answer she was waiting for. "Laura took it quite differently from what I expected," he said. "She was awfully decent about it. I think she was relieved, in a way, to find she had not got me on her mind. She must have been afraid I should be very unhappy, of course. She would always be so sorry about anything like that, that I wonder she had the heart to throw me over, even though she didn't want me."

Caroline said nothing. Oddly enough, though she had not heard the sound of the waves before, the melancholy swish! swish! now echoed through her very soul. When she felt a salt taste on her lips she thought it was a drop of spray from the sea, then she felt the faint trickling sensation of another and another running down her cheeks.

"Caroline!" he said, putting his arm about her and bending his face to hers. "You're crying! What is it, little girl?"

She pulled herself away from him, sobbing out with a wild earnestness which he found incomprehensible: "No! No! You can't start yet. You have her kisses on your mouth yet."

"You didn't seem to mind that before," he said, suddenly white with anger. "I don't know why you should start to be jealous of Laura now everything is over."

"I'm not jealous," she said. "It is not that." Then she stopped short. He must believe what he liked, for she could not betray the secret of a girl whose love, she felt, was finer than her own.

"Well, you have no need to be jealous," he said. "She spoke nicely about you. She was awfully decent about it, and hoped you and she would be friends."

"Oh! I wish we could be," said Caroline, but deep down in her own consciousness she knew this would never happen; because it is not in human nature for a woman to cease being jealous of another who has done more than herself for the man she loves.

He stood there disconsolately, kicking a pebble. He had come hot-foot to claim her, never anticipating a check; and now she seemed to be somehow drifting farther and farther away from him.

"I don't know if you are still thinking about the money Laura lent me," he said at last. "I begin to wish now I hadn't told you. But I wanted to have everything quite straight." He paused. "As a matter of fact, I have paid it back. The bank was a bit awkward at first, but I was able to come to an arrangement with them a day or two ago, and I have repaid Laura what she lent me." He paused again, looking at her almost comically: "There, I hope you quite understand?"

They were indeed talking to each other more like enemies than lovers; and Caroline seemed to be more than ever withdrawn and aloof—for all her ignorance and simplicity of feeling—when she answered him in an inward brooding tone: "Yes, I understand." For she really saw neither Godfrey nor the shore, only Laura coming flushed out of the door marked "Private" behind the bank counter. For now—at last—she did see where it all led. She had to join issue with Laura to spare the pride of this man whom both loved. His faith in his own power of overcoming difficulties was the foundation on which his life was built, and they must not pull it from under him. She, at any rate, could not so humiliate him.

"The difficulty was only temporary," he went on, trying to find out what she was waiting for. "I tried to do too much business for my capital. But I'm bound to get on. We shall be all right."

"Don't!" she said sharply. "I don't care about money. I wasn't thinking about that."

"Then what's the matter?"

She looked at him dumbly, and something in her tear-stained face tugged irresistibly at his heartstrings. "Don't look like that," he said. "Let's forget all that has happened before. You don't mean you will turn me down, too?"

She shook her head, still unable to keep back the tears.

"Then why are you crying?" he said, putting his arm round her. "There's nothing to cry for, Carrie." He spoke to her soothingly, tenderly, as a man might to a child who was in trouble.

"Oh, Godfrey!" She drew herself away from him once more. "I aren't half as good as her. I aren't half as good as her. You'd have been a great deal happier and more comfortable with her."

"I know that," he said. "But I don't want to be happy and comfortable. I want to live." He caught hold of her hand, which he crushed so tightly that it hurt. "And I want you with me."

They heard a sudden noise from the cliff top where two boys raced and shouted, so they walked on. Feathery clots of foam blew before them on the sand, almost as if sea-flowers from the changeless ocean were being flung in the pathway of that which is unchangeable in human life.

After a while Caroline said with a start, waking out of her dream: "I wonder what Mrs. Bradford will say? But she won't be so upset as Miss Ethel would have been." She lowered her voice. "Do you know what Miss Panton said it was that actually killed Miss Ethel? It was everything being so different."

"Yes." He paused. "Well, thousands of people are dying from the same cause, I suppose, all over the world—middle-aged ones, that is." Then he strengthened his grasp on her arm. "But we're young. We're all right. Eh, Caroline?"

THE END

Milton Keynes UK
Ingram Content Group UK Ltd.
UKHW030719041024
449263UK00004B/382